Night Fires

Joan Lingard

PUFFIN BOOKS

For Jane Nissen

PUFFIN BOOKS

Published by the Penguin Group
Penguin Books Ltd, 27 Wrights Lane, London W8 5TZ, England
Penguin Books USA Inc., 375 Hudson Street, New York, New York 10014, USA
Penguin Books Australia Ltd, Ringwood, Victoria, Australia
Penguin Books Canada Ltd, 10 Alcorn Avenue, Toronto, Ontario, Canada M4V 3B2
Penguin Books (NZ) Ltd, 182–190 Wairau Road, Auckland 10, New Zealand

Penguin Books Ltd, Registered Offices: Harmondsworth, Middlesex, England

First published by Hamish Hamilton 1993
Published in Puffin Books 1995
1 3 5 7 9 10 8 6 4 2

Copyright © Joan Lingard, 1993
All rights reserved

The moral right of the author has been asserted

Filmset in Monophoto Times
Printed in England by Clays Ltd, St Ives plc

SUNDAY: *MIDNIGHT*

For three nights running, Lara dreamed a dream of burning, of buildings blazing, and flames leaping into the sky. On the third night, she was wakened by Nik shaking her and saying, 'Get up, Lara, the city's on fire!'

She leapt up, startled, with the taste of smoke in her mouth. Nik was standing beside her bed, fully clothed. In the long shadowy room, lit by a solitary feeble night-light, the other children slept on in their narrow truckle beds. Some shifted restlessly with their arms flung above their heads, others were moaning, calling out for people who were not there. There was terror in their cries. Dreams seared their sleep. Vivid, disturbing dreams. Few escaped them.

Nik left her and crossed to the window. It stuck part-way when he tried to push it up and he had to put his shoulder to it. He waited to see if the noise had disturbed anyone, then he put out his head and leaned his elbows on the sill. Lara tiptoed over the bare floor to join him. The wooden boards felt cool and jagged beneath her feet. He shifted to make room for her.

'Look!' He pointed at the horizon, in the direction of the city.

The sky glowed with a weird light, a wild orange-red in colour. It looked as if the whole of the heavens was lit up. You could almost believe that the world was coming to an end. Lara shivered. The sharp scent of burning reached them on the night air.

They frowned, and looked questioningly at each other. The city was several kilometres away. Could the smell of smoke travel that far? It seemed to be coming from somewhere nearer at hand, almost underneath them, in fact. Their noses twitched.

Leaning further out they saw, directly below in the courtyard, two figures tending a bonfire. They were able to make out the scene clearly, for overhead an almost full butter-yellow moon had come sailing out from behind a bank of cloud. The two were fuelling the bonfire with boxes and armfuls of paper. They were working feverishly, like people gripped by panic. One – the man – was tall and thin and wore a long black coat and black boots. He was easily recognisable. He was the director of the orphanage. They called him the Crow not only because he dressed in black, but also on account of his long arms that he flapped like wings before he swooped. His companion was the matron, who was squat and fat, and known as Dracula.

'What are they doing?' whispered Lara.

'Burning papers. Files, I suspect.'

The smell was acrid now and smoke was rising thick and black like a plume into the air, making their eyes sting. With a lunge the Crow flung the last box onto the flames. As soon as it was engulfed it caught fire and burned brightly for a few brief

2

moments before it blackened and began to disintegrate. The director stood back from the blaze, watching closely, as if to make sure that not a scrap survived, then he wiped his hands down the sides of his black coat. Dracula nodded. Together they turned and came back into the building.

'They might come up and find us.' Lara drew in her head. The Crow and Dracula would be furious if they were to catch them out of bed. Unconsciously, she touched the bruise on her arm, where the matron had seized her only that morning. Dracula's temper was fiendish. She would take their flesh between her fingers and nip until they flinched or cried out. Her fingers were like pincers. Lara made it a point of honour not to cry out, not to give the woman satisfaction, which meant of course that she would pinch even harder.

'Perhaps we should go back to bed, Nik.'

'Somehow I don't think they're going to be interested in us tonight. I think they've got other things on their minds. Yes, here they come again!'

The pair had re-emerged from the doorway below. They were each carrying a suitcase in one hand and in the other, a large duffel bag with zip gaping open and the contents spilling out. Their shoulders were pulled down by the weight. They lumbered across the courtyard to where the director's black car stood.

'I think they've left the door open!' said Lara. The heavy studded door was always kept locked and double-barred at night, often even in the daytime. 'They didn't stop to lock it.'

The director and matron flung their luggage into

3

the boot of the car, tried to shut the lid, failed, left it cocked up in the air, and hastened round to the front. They clambered in. He took the wheel, she sat hunched forward in the passenger seat, her nose almost touching the windscreen. Lara and Nik listened while the Crow tried to start the engine. It coughed, died, coughed again, and died even more quickly. The director cursed.

'He could be out of petrol,' murmured Nik.

Petrol, like food and other forms of fuel, was scarce. People queued at lay-bys, on the off-chance, in case a tanker might happen to come along and sell them a can or two. They would wait for hours at a time. Sometimes they had to abandon their cars because their tanks were empty.

Much trade was done on the black market. The Crow was known to be a big black-marketeer in the district. Men arrived at the orphanage in vans at dead of night and carried in boxes by the back door. They brought in everything from transistors and television sets to dead chickens and cans of petrol. Then other vans would come and take the stuff away. The Crow kept his money in a locked iron safe in his room. Biba, the old nurse who was in charge of the babies, said he insisted on being paid in foreign currency: dollars, pounds sterling, Deutschmarks, francs. The currency of their own country was worthless.

Nik and Lara learned a great many things from Biba. She herself got news of the outside world from her grandson Oscar whose parents were dead and whom she had brought up. He was a university student and a dissident, which meant that he was against the

4

harsh regime that ruled their country. He opposed it openly, not under his breath, behind closed doors, the way most people did, scared that they might be taken away in the night by the Secret Police. Oscar spent much of his time in hiding, moving from one 'safe house' in the city to another. Biba worried constantly about him.

The Crow was trying the engine again. Once more it spluttered and expired and once more he swore. His window was open and his right arm rested on the ledge. He slapped the outside panel of the door with his hand. He was getting angry.

Please let them have enough petrol, Lara prayed inside her head, please let them just *go*! They couldn't be out of petrol surely, not *them*. If there was something else wrong with the car that would be more serious, for new parts were difficult to come by. They were said to be as rare as gold dust.

Nik was thinking what a pity it was that he couldn't go down and give them a push. In his imagination he put out his hands and shoved hard, and at that very moment, as if he had willed it, the engine hiccuped one more time and burst suddenly and noisily into life. Nik gave a quiet cheer.

Clanking and backfiring, the old car puttered across the courtyard and began to slither down the muddy, rutted drive to the main road. Lara and Nik watched with fingers crossed.

When the car reached the end of the drive it waited there, throbbing, while the matron bobbed out and ran to open the high iron gates. Her arms were at full stretch as she pushed them aside. Then she jumped back in and even before she had slammed her door shut the car was edging forward again, putting its nose out into the road. It turned right in the direction of the main highway. Its lights flickered behind the tall trees that bordered the orphanage grounds. Then the rumble of the engine gradually began to recede. Lara and Nik strained to listen. The noise grew fainter and fainter.

Lara lifted her head. 'It's gone. *They've* gone! Can you believe it, Nik? They've actually *gone*?'

'Get dressed! Quickly!'

'Buy why? It's late.' Lara looked at her watch, which had once belonged to her father. It was twenty minutes after midnight.

'We're going out.'

'*Out*?'

'Yes, out!'

MONDAY: *12.20 a.m.*

It was seldom that they left the orphanage, especially on their own. They did not even go to the school in the nearby village; teachers came in and gave them lessons. They went out only on organised outings, to museums and factories. Then they would travel by hired coach. There had been few of these trips in recent months.

'Yes, we're going out, Lara,' repeated Nik.

He darted across the landing to the boys' dormitory to fetch his anorak. Quickly Lara threw off her night-dress and pulled on underclothes, tee-shirt, trousers, sweater, socks, trainers, anorak. The sweater and anorak were grey, like Nik's, like all the other children's in the orphanage; and the trousers were black.

'Ready?'

Nik was standing in the doorway, poised for take-off. Lara took a last look at the sleeping children. In the bed beside her own slept Katya, who was five years old and a special favourite of hers. 'I'll be back,' she whispered, though Katya would not hear. Katya would want to know when and Lara would not have been able to give her an answer. Everything was uncertain at present. Life was changing. There had been a great deal of unrest in the city, and in the countryside too. Biba had kept abreast of the news.

People had been gathering in large numbers to protest against the regime. Not even the strong-armed tactics of the police had deterred them. For years they had been ruled by a President – a dictator – who had kept them screwed down under his iron thumb, as had his father before him. Hundreds of protestors had been arrested. But you can't arrest a whole nation, said Biba. What do you do with them? Shoot them? There comes a point when people would rather die than put up with more suffering. There comes a point when they are determined to have their freedom.

Lara slipped her hand under her pillow and took out the little waterproof packet that held the photographs of her parents. One had been taken on their wedding day, the other was of herself as a baby in her mother's arms. The sun was shining and they were sitting under an apple tree. It must have been early summer for the tree was frothy with blossom. Her father was standing behind them, with his hands

7

on her mother's shoulders, smiling. The photographs were Lara's most precious possessions.

She was lucky, she could still remember her parents. Many of the orphanage children could not. She remembered her father as being handsome, brave and upright when he went off with the Secret Police. He had kept his dignity. They had come for him in the middle of the night, the way they always came for people. The loud knock on the door had chilled their hearts. There had been no time for their father to run. He had been living in a 'safe house', had returned home only the evening before. Had someone betrayed him? They never found out.

Before they took him away, he had kissed Lara and said, 'Take care of your mother for me. Take care of one another!' She thought he knew he would not come back. Then he walked out of the room between the two black-bereted men. They never saw him alive again.

The police tortured and shot him and dumped him on waste ground nearby. Lara and her mother brought home his body. He had felt heavy and limp. His head lolled in her mother's arms. Blood caked his face. The priest helped to bury him, secretly, in an old cemetery on the outskirts of the town, in the grave where his parents lay. Shortly afterwards, Lara's mother, whose health had never been good, fell ill and died also. She had wanted to lie with her husband, everyone said. Her wish had been fulfilled. That had been three years ago.

'Lara!'

'Coming!' Lara put the waterproof packet into her anorak pocket.

'Lara!' A second voice was calling her, a small, frightened voice. Katya had wakened and was sitting up, rubbing her eyes. 'Where are you going, Lara? Are you going out?'

'Just for a little while.'

'Don't go! Take me! Take me with you!' Katya held out her arms.

'I can't, Katya.' Lara put her arms round the child and hugged her. 'It's late. It's dark outside.'

'Lara!' Nik signalled from the doorway.

'I must go, Katya.' Lara tried to disentangle herself from the child's arms.

Katya began to cry and to cling more tightly.

'I'll be back, Katya, I promise.' Lara kissed her and wrenched herself free.

Closing her ears to Katya's sobs, she ran after Nik, following him down the stairs on to the next landing. From the nursery came the sound of babies crying.

They pushed open the door. The room, like their dormitories, was dark except for the light shed by one night-lamp. In the pool of pale light sat Biba on a low chair, rocking two babies, one on either arm. She had been crooning to them. She looked up at Nik and Lara, showing no surprise at seeing them fully dressed.

They squatted in front of her.

'We're going out, Biba,' said Nik.

Biba nodded.

'*They* have gone,' said Lara.

'I know. They had to run, like rats! To save their skins. I could smell the fear on their breath at supper time. They knew their time was up. Let's hope that it is!'

9

'Will you be all right on your own?' asked Lara. They would be leaving Biba alone with twenty children, most of them under the age of five. 'You don't mind us going?'

'I realize you want to go – to be there when something important is happening. But take care how you do go! You mustn't get too close to the trouble. So go and look, but stay back! Do you hear what old Biba is telling you? Don't be like that hot-headed grandson of mine, Oscar!' She spoke, though, with pride. 'You must see to it that Nik's head doesn't get too hot, Lara.'

'I don't think hers stays all that cool at times!' Nik grinned as Lara punched him lightly on the upper arm.

'If you need to take shelter somewhere, you can always go to my sister Nina's house. You would be most welcome there. She lives on Birch Street, number twenty-seven. That's east of the Markets area of the city.'

In turn, they kissed Biba's soft wrinkled cheek that smelled of the babies she was nursing.

'God go with you!' she said, and went back to rocking the babies.

Nik and Lara closed the nursery door behind them, then down the next flight of stairs they went, their feet skimming the treads as if winged. There was no sound of anyone moving on the ground floor. The kitchen and cleaning staff lived out, in the village.

The moon shone in through the open doorway, sending a streak of light across the stone-flagged hall floor. The smell of the night air was sweet after the sour orphanage smell of disinfectant, stale urine and unwashed clothes. They stood for a moment on the step, breathing in the sharp cold air, letting their eyes rest on the rosy sky that capped the horizon.

Then they caught hands and began to run, away from the high, gloomy brick building, towards the burning city.

MONDAY: *1 a.m.*

After a while they were forced to stop. They had stitches in their sides and their breathing had become quick and jerky. They gulped in great lungfuls of air and rubbed their sides, before setting off again, this time at a brisk walking pace. They were glad of the moon to light their way. Their legs moved with a steady rhythm, and they kept in step with one another.

They were on the main highway that ran into the city, but on this stretch of road there were few houses. They passed a tumble-down cottage with a caved-in roof, a slew of rusted car chassis and abandoned tractors in a field, and a farmhouse shuttered and dark. A dog lifted its square head and howled as they went by. They hurried past.

They were coming along the side of a thick pine wood when they saw pinpricks of light appear up ahead. Moving pinpricks, growing larger every second. They stopped. Now they could make out the low hum of a car engine.

'It can't be them, can it?' said Lara. 'Not coming *back*?'

The headlights were travelling fast towards them.

'It looks like an army truck!' yelled Nik, squinting into the blinding lights.'Quickly!'

He seized Lara's arm and dragged her into the edge of the wood. They flung themselves face down in the undergrowth.

The truck roared to a squealing halt, and the near-side door shot open. Out leapt an officer wearing high, gleaming, black boots. He was looking in their direction.

'Who is there?' he called.

'Let's go!' said Nik.

They jumped to their feet and dove into the dark interior of the wood.

'Halt!' cried the officer, but they did not look round.

They kept their backs bent and their heads down. A shot rang out. They went floundering on, thrusting aside branches that clawed at their faces and tried to bar their way. Their shins banged against fallen tree stumps, their ankles turned on unseen, spiky stones. The wood was like an enemy to be fought, yet it was their friend, their only hope.

Pausing briefly to listen they heard the sound of crashing feet and raised voices not far behind them. They had been followed into the wood.

They *must* find a path. They couldn't go blundering on like this. The trees were so close together they were interlocked. Their eyes, though, were beginning to adjust to the change of light. Peering through the trees Nik thought he could detect a break in them.

'Lara, this way!' He beckoned.

Turning she saw a long avenue cutting a swathe

through the trees to make a clear pathway, lit by moonlight.

They made for the vee-shaped opening, and on reaching it, began to run again. They ran as fast as they could ever remember running. The path, cushioned with old pine needles, was soft under their feet.

When they found they could run no more, they collapsed on to a mound of spongy sphagnum moss. They gasped for breath. Their legs twitched from the exertion.

Gradually the pounding of their hearts subsided, and the world around them stilled.

They must have dropped off briefly to sleep, for they came to, wondering where they were. The wind was muttering in the tops of the trees above their heads. 'Go home,' it seemed to be saying. 'Go home!' They breathed in deeply. The air had a spicy tang, compounded of scents of pine and resin and damp earth.

They sat up and Lara released her long dark hair from its ribbon. Dracula had threatened often to cut it; she hated the girls to have long hair. Once, when she had advanced with scissors in her hand, Lara had turned on her with such venom that even she had retreated. She had looked almost frightened, as if she thought Lara might seize the scissors and plunge them into her soft body. Lara had been determined to keep her hair. It was like having a luxury, something special that was hers and hers alone. She remembered sitting in front of her mother's knees by the fire and her mother brushing her hair, one stroke after the other, gently, gently. She remembered falling asleep.

13

Lara let her hair swirl around her neck and shoulders, before tying it back again.

'We seem to have lost them,' she said.

'We'd better lie low for a while, just in case they're still hanging around.'

'What would they want with us?'

'What do they want with anybody?'

'But they *shot* at us.'

'Probably because we ran.'

'Perhaps we shouldn't have?'

'You know we had to, Lara. We have no identification papers.'

Their papers would be in the orphanage safe, unless they had been burnt along with the other records the Crow had been stuffing into the fire. Without papers you could be arrested and locked up. On the other hand, thought Lara, the soldiers might have taken them back to the orphanage. And that might not have been as bad as sitting in the middle of a black wood in damp, clammy clothes, not knowing whether soldiers were waiting for you to show yourself so that they could take pot shots at you.

It felt strange to be outside at night, surrounded by things they could not see. They were used to walls around them. There could be wolves lurking in the wood. Or evil spirits. Biba had told them folk tales about spirits, both good and bad, who inhabited the primeval forests. She had told them about children who had come into these forests never to be seen again. She said they were happy in the secret places that they found.

Lara was not so sure about that. She would not

want to stay in here for ever. She could believe that unseen eyes were watching them, glinting in the darkness. Glinting gleefully. Enjoying their discomfort. Something rustled behind them. A shiver ran up her spine and she glanced first over one shoulder and then the other. Some of the trees looked like witches, the way they were hunched over and holding out their skinny arms.

'I wonder how Biba's getting on,' she said. She thought of the nursery and the curtains drawn against the night.

'She'll be okay.'

'Perhaps we should have stayed and helped her.'

'Perhaps, perhaps! We're here now, not there. But you can go back if you want to.'

MONDAY: *2 a.m.*

Oh, could she indeed? Nik's voice had been cool. Lara hated it when he went cold on her. Well, okay, if he wanted to be like that then let him! She got up and moved a few steps up the path, away from him.

When Nik was annoyed, or upset about something, he would clamp up tight, like a hedgehog rolling itself into a ball at the hint of danger. He would become prickly and silent. She hated his silence. He didn't talk about things as easily as she did, especially if they were troubling.

All the orphanage children had pasts that troubled them; they wouldn't be there otherwise. Some talked about them and let the tears come; others remained dry-eyed and tight-lipped. Each person coped in his

15

or her own way, said Biba. On the whole the boys talked less than the girls, and tried to hold back their tears. They seemed to feel they had to be strong. But, as Biba said, there were different ways of being strong.

Nik was one of the tight-lipped brigade. His mother had died when he was eight and his father, like Lara's, had been arrested by the Black Berets, the special police force. Nik's father had been taken to the infamous top security jail in the city, which housed political prisoners, most of whom were held without trial. Lara wondered if Nik had been so anxious to go into the city tonight because of his father. She wished he would just *say*. She didn't even know if he still thought of his father. When she asked him about his early life, he'd shrug and turn the conversation to something else. He'd even become offhand for a while, as he was being now. The past was past, he said. Surely nobody could believe that? Didn't you carry it with you, inside you? How could you ever leave it totally behind? It had made you what you were.

Yet in spite of all that, Lara felt close to Nik and thought of him as her best friend. They did most things together. They were two years older than any other child at the orphanage.

At this moment, though, she did not feel too friendly towards him! Why did he have to go all huffy on her now? Especially on a night such as this? A night when the world was turning itself upside down and inside out and they were adrift together in a thick, dark wood.

Lara sighed, turned and went back to him. It was always she who had to make the first move, to be the one to bridge the gap. Sometimes she thought he wanted to, but couldn't. She looked up into his thin, shadowy face, partly lit by moonlight. His eyes were unreadable. His brows were knotted.

'Shall I come with you?' she asked.

'If you like.'

'What do *you* like?'

He glanced away from her dark, flashing eyes. Even in the moonlight he could see that they flashed. She seemed to be angry with him. He couldn't make out what went on in her head at times. He knew she would say that he did not try to. They would be getting along well together and then without warning everything would shift and he would not be able to follow her changing mood. Of course he wanted her to come with him! She must know that. So why was she asking? Hadn't he wakened her up, told her to get dressed, to *come*? Did she really think he would let her go back to the orphanage in the dark, alone? She was playing games with him. At a time like this!

'Well?' She was waiting for an answer.

'You're being silly.'

'If that's what you think!'

'Wait!' He caught hold of her arm. 'Lara, I want you to come.'

Finding a way back out to the road was not easy. The wood was like a tortuous maze, a bewildering, confusing place, alive with the noise of snapping twigs, branches creaking and sighing in the wind, and small unseen scurrying animals. At one point a large shape sprang across the path in front of them and went crashing into the trees. Lara drew back, petrified, in case it might be a wolf, but Nik thought it was probably a deer.

'Wolves stand their ground. Deer run.'

'You're just saying that! I saw its eyes. They were like lamps.'

'You're imagining things!'

When finally they did emerge from the wood, they found they had come out at a different place from where they had entered. The sky would have to be their guide. Above the city, it was crimson.

As they drew closer to the outlying suburbs, the smell of smoke thickened. A grey pall was drifting over the rooftops and the air was full of small dark particles. The moon looked blood-coloured now, and had a blurred ring around it.

They came to a stretch of waste ground on which a rash of bonfires threw up sparks against the night sky. They passed a block of high flats, boasting on its side a monstrous portrait of the President. It must have been four or five storeys high. His face was everywhere in the country, on billboards, the sides of buildings: a heavy-jowled face, with thick, black eyebrows that met in the middle and a broad, flat nose, with wide nostrils. It was a face that made people lower their gaze as they went by. It was a face that made them shudder if they looked up.

The streets were busy. It was difficult to believe it was the middle of the night. People thronged the pavements, coming and going, or standing about in groups of two, three, four and more, talking, gesticulating. On corners men and women huddled around smoking braziers warming their hands. There seemed to be fire everywhere.

Nik and Lara walked steadily on towards the city centre, not tired at all now, in spite of the lateness of the hour and their lack of sleep.

They came to a halt at a traffic light. While they waited a convoy of four tanks with closed hatches ground slowly past, then came a police car racing through the red light, just as the pedestrians were getting ready to cross. Its four occupants stared straight ahead. They did not seem to want to look at the people in the street. They did not even blink when their car hit a pot-hole and threw them forward in their seats. The streets were full of pot-holes, just as the pavements were fragmented and in a poor state of repair.

'I heard some of the municipal buildings had been fired,' a woman beside Lara said to her companion. 'And several warehouses in the south of the city.' The woman's voice was excited, and tinged with fear.

The municipal buildings – the City Hall and its offices – were in Cathedral Square, right in the heart of the old mediaeval city.

The walking man symbol lit up, and the crowd moved forward. Nik and Lara went with it, part of it now; they were no longer on their own. They felt themselves being borne along by its energy. It was like being picked up by a tidal wave. They joined hands again. It would be easy to lose one another. All the time more and more people were joining on, and the crowd was swelling.

Near the centre, the streets narrowed. The buildings here were old, mostly narrow-fronted and painted in varying shades of blue, green, clay-red and ochre, a welcome change from the greyness of the new, outer suburbs. People filled the roadway and the thin strips of pavement from wall to wall.

They surged on to the humped-back bridge that straddled the river and would take them on to the square. The air was loud with the chant of voices.

Freedom! We want our freedom!

On the corner of the square, they stopped. The vast space in front of them was filled with people.

Then they saw the riot police.

MONDAY: *4 a.m.*

Clad in helmets of blue-grey steel, riot shields in their left hands, batons in their right, the police ringed the square. At the far end, smoke was issuing from the police headquarters and three municipal office blocks. The roof of one building had collapsed. Firemen wielding hoses were swarming up and down long ladders, looking like yellow ants. They had brought the fires almost under control. The City Hall, a fine seventeenth-century stone building with elaborately carved balconies, appeared to be untouched, as did the equally splendid Gothic cathedral which dominated the square. From the City Hall flew the red and black flag of the regime.

The building whose roof had caved in was the Ministry of Information. It was one of the most hated buildings in the city, in the whole country. No wonder the students had fired that! It was the headquarters of the Secret Service and the Secret Police.

And behind it was the top security jail. Lara remembered walking past the prison with her mother. They would quicken their steps until they had left the high, forbidding stone wall behind. Terrible things went on in there, Lara's mother had told her. She had been glad they had not locked her husband up in such a place. Better to die and lie in the quiet earth. They couldn't touch you there.

The huge crowd in the square moved restlessly, swaying and chanting. And every now and then they let out an enormous roar of *Freedom*!

'Come on, Lara,' urged Nik. 'Let's try and get closer to the front.'

He plunged into the midst of the crowd, pulling Lara after him. He squeezed between people, ducked under arms, trod on feet, was cursed, but pressed on, muttering apologies. Lara followed, clinging desperately to Nik's hand. She knew that when he made up his mind he wanted to go somewhere he would let nothing stop him.

They came to a halt five or six rows back from the City Hall. Here the crowd was even denser; no one would give up his or her position. They could move neither forwards nor backwards. They saw that the front four rows were taken up by students who stood with their feet planted apart and arms linked right along the line.

Facing them was a row of armed police.

'Isn't that Oscar in the front row?' Lara stood up on her toes to make sure. She was right! Oscar's red hair, flaming like a beacon and worn long, down over his collar, was distinctive. She and Nik had met him on several occasions in Biba's room. He came always at night, when he would first have made sure that the Crow and Dracula were away on one of their little jaunts. They went every few weeks to big country houses that were kept as holiday resorts for friends of the regime.

Lara wondered where the two of them would be now. She had a vision of the old black car crouching at the roadside like a broken-backed beetle, and the director and matron scuttling across a field, dragging their suitcases behind them.

Oscar had heard her. He glanced round fleetingly and gave them a quick smile and a nod.

The police waited with firearms presented, aimed straight at the students' chests. Their fingers rested on the barrels of the guns, ready to slide that last centimetre along the cold steel and pull back the triggers. And unleash a hail of death. It would be so easy. And it could happen so fast. In the blink of an eye. Lara shuddered and linked her fingers through Nik's. His arm was trembling too.

'Will they shoot, do you think?' she whispered.

'They might.'

The man on Nik's other side spoke to them. 'They will if the students charge. The students want to take over the City Hall. I hear they've been trying to occupy the TV station. There are many rumours going around, of course.' He shrugged. 'Who knows what is true these days? Who has ever known? We have been fed lies all our lives.'

'But the students would never get through the police lines,' said Lara. 'How could they? They're not armed.'

'It would certainly be a desperate move. But these

22

are desperate times. And the police might *not* shoot. They say that many of them are sick of the regime, too. Well, they're people, aren't they? Human beings. Part of us, when all is said and done.'

'Some are monsters,' said another man. 'When you think of some of the things they have done!'

So much has changed so quickly, Nik was thinking. Here he and Lara were, standing in the middle of a huge crowd, listening to two men speak against the government! They were not even lowering their voices. All around them people were saying similar things. Yet they had always been cautioned never to speak against the regime in public, and certainly not to a stranger, who might work for the Secret Police. Even when talking to a friend you had to remember there were bugging devices everywhere. When you grew up in a police state you learned these things at an early age.

Suddenly there was a stir up on the main balcony of the City Hall. Something was about to happen. The crowd quietened. All eyes swept upward.

The back door of the balcony opened and out stepped a policeman with gold epaulettes and heavily gold-braided hat. He was accompanied by four armed men wearing black leather jerkins and trousers and black berets. The Black Berets stood two on either side of the gold-bedecked policeman, pointing their sub-machine guns down into the crowd.

'The Chief of Police,' muttered Nik's neighbour.

The police chief raised a tannoy to his mouth and addressed them.

'Citizens, I appeal to you to leave the square and go home peaceably. Go home now before there is any bloodshed! You are here because a handful of student dissidents – traitors! – are trying to cause trouble. I suggest that you do not want trouble. But if you do, then you shall have it. So I give you this warning: leave of your own accord now or else I shall give orders to my men to clear you from the square!'

He lowered the tannoy, and whipped around on his heel, his grey greatcoat swirling over the tops of his high boots. He left the balcony, followed by his bodyguards. The door swung to behind them.

For a moment there was a hush in the square, then a babble of voices broke out. One came over the top of all the others, also speaking through a tannoy. Looking round they saw that a student had mounted a lamp-post. Other students stood below him, supporting his arms and legs.

'Stand firm, friends, I beseech you! Don't go! Don't let them win again! We've suffered enough. Our parents have suffered and our grandparents. Now is the time to stand firm –'

A sharp report rang out. It might have been the backfiring of a car, except that there were no cars in the square to be seen or heard. The student had slumped forward, a look of surprise on his face. Then he slid down the lamp-post, and the other students fell back, equally surprised, and totally horrified.

MONDAY: 5 a.m.

Panic ensued. People screamed, pushed, ran, tripped, floundered, fell. Police charged, batons flailed, shields drove into terrified faces. Nik and Lara were tossed about in the midst of the seething crowd like flotsam in a turbulent sea, scarcely able to keep their feet. Further shots rang out. The crowd pushed harder, trying to reach the narrow exits out of the square.

A man went down in front of Lara and in the next instant, unable to stop herself, she felt herself falling. She went sprawling face downward over the top of his body. She saw the ground coming up to meet her. She felt the breath being knocked from her chest.

Hands seized her shoulders. They were Nik's hands, thin but strong from all the hard physical work they'd had to do at the orphanage. They hauled her up, out of the nightmare tangle of threshing legs and kicking feet. Her face surfaced, her feet found the ground. She gulped. Her head rocked, and she thought she was going to be sick.

'Take a deep breath,' Nik yelled into her ear. 'Okay?'

She nodded and breathed in, then out. Her ribs felt as if they were on fire. She took another deep breath and her head cleared, just a little, though her eyes were still unable to focus.

Nik put his arm around her waist, and she steadied. Keeping close together, forming a bulwark to withstand the force of the crowd's movement, they managed to reach the side of the square, where they fell back against the wall of the cathedral. They rested there in its shadow, breathing hard. The building had been deconsecrated by the regime and was used now as a museum.

The large space in front of them was emptying fast; people were fleeing in every direction. The only ones not running were a posse of Black Berets and some twenty to thirty students. The students had been arrested. They walked stiffly with their hands held high above their heads and as they walked they were prodded in the back by guns and bayonets.

Lara put her hands over her face. Her shoulders shook. She was crying, Nik knew. His own throat felt tight and dry. What could he say to her that would comfort her? He couldn't tell her that everything would be all right. It looked as if nothing in their poor country would ever be all right. The dictator and his henchmen had won yet again.

Nik touched Lara's shoulder. 'We must go. We can't stay here.'

She dried her eyes on the back of her hand, and went with him. It was a night in which it seemed that the running would never stop.

Rounding a corner, coming into a quiet side street, they saw up ahead a young man with a university scarf trailing from his neck. He was half carrying, half dragging a wounded fellow student along the pavement and making little progress. He stopped to lean against the wall of a baker's shop. This was a street of small shops, shuttered and dark at this hour. Even in the daytime many would remain closed, having nothing to sell.

As they drew level with the students, Nik and Lara recognized the wounded one. It was Oscar! His scarf had been wrapped around his head in an effort to conceal a wound. Blood trickled from his matted red hair down his temple. His eyes were closed. The other student was wounded too, on his upper arm.

'Is he all right?' Lara ran forward and knelt down beside Oscar. 'Nik, he looks bad!'

'Can we help?' asked Nik. 'Oscar's a friend of ours.'

'Please, would you?' The student sounded on the verge of collapse. 'Can you take him from me?'

'But what about you? You need help, too.'

'I'll manage. But I can't carry Oscar any further. Need to get away from here,' he muttered. He glanced back down the street. 'Before the police come.'

They took Oscar from his arms into theirs. His head lolled, reminding Lara of that terrible journey she and her mother had made through the streets with her dead father. She thought for a moment she might faint. Take another deep breath! she told herself. This is not a time for fainting. Her head cleared.

This man was not her father. It was Oscar whom they held, and he was still alive. *He* mustn't be allowed to die. His breathing was uneven and his face a dreadful pallid white, the colour of soiled linen, tinged with blue around the mouth and nose.

Oscar's friend staggered off, keeping close to the walls, putting out a hand every few metres to steady himself. Behind him on the pavement he left a trail of red blots.

For a few seconds Nik and Lara stayed where they were, not knowing what to do or in which direction to go. They looked helplessly at one another over Oscar's inert body. Nik held his head and shoulders, Lara his feet. His body was buckling in the middle, his bottom scraping the pavement. His dead weight was heavy.

Each knew what the other was thinking. If they were to carry Oscar away, and help him to escape from the police, they would no longer be onlookers, spectators. They would be involved and would be counted amongst the dissidents. Enemies of the state. And they would thus be in grave danger themselves.

MONDAY: *DAWN*

'We're already involved,' said Nik.

Lara nodded.

They looked round. People – men – were shouting, somewhere not far away.

'We'd better get out of here,' said Nik. 'Ready, Lara?'

They managed to raise Oscar a little higher off the ground. He felt as heavy and unmanageable as a sack of wet cement. With Nik leading they set off, following the red-spotted trail left by the other student. They lurched along, swinging wildly from side to side.

When they reached the corner they turned into another, similar street of shops with battened-down shutters. Half the street lights were dark and the shadows between were dense. Nothing appeared to be stirring.

'Hang on a moment, Nik!' said Lara, and he stopped and looked back. 'Where are we going?' she asked.

'I don't know!'

Lara had a sudden thought. 'What about Biba's sister?'

Of course! It was the obvious place to go. The only possible place.

Birch Street, Biba had said. Number twenty-seven. East of the Markets area. But how were they to find that at this hour of the morning and with no one around whom they could ask?

They would just have to press on, said Nik, in the hope that they might find someone who could help them. A student perhaps, going home. The main thing was to get clear of the city centre, since this was where police activity would be greatest. They would be arresting known dissidents and picking up stragglers.

'We'd certainly qualify as stragglers!' said Lara.

They could make no speed at all. They trailed to the end of the street and down the next one, resting every few metres, keeping their eyes and ears on constant alert. Whenever they heard a car approaching they bundled Oscar into a doorway and stood in front of him. The two vehicles that did go by seemed to be civilian; they had no lights and went screeching down the street, exceeding the speed limit, paying no attention whatsoever to them.

They covered another few metres, and then they heard a police siren. This one was coming their way.

Looking round they quickly took stock. Beside them was a wide, half broken-down gate. They pushed it open to find themselves in a builder's yard. There were no materials in it, or none that they could see, only rubbish, making strange shapes in the moonlight. They dragged Oscar inside, propped him against the wall and slumped down themselves, one on either side of him.

Oscar's eyelids fluttered, and he moaned. At least he was still alive. They positioned an arm each behind his head, in order to cushion it and make him a little more comfortable.

On the other side of the wall, the street was filling up with noise. First came the wail of sirens, then the roar of motor bikes and car engines, followed by the stamp of running feet and blare of raised voices. The cacophony of sound did not disturb them. They listened to it dully. They had reached a point of exhaustion when they almost did not care if the police were to burst in and seize them.

The sirens cut out, but the rest of the commotion continued. More voices joined the fray. There seemed to be some sort of scuffle going on. Now came a shout of triumph. *Got him*! The police must have been in pursuit of someone else, not them. And they had run him to earth.

Car doors slammed, bang, bang, bang, one after the other, in rapid succession. The noise of revving engines swelled, then they began to move away, and after a few minutes there was silence in the street.

A bluish light was beginning to seep into the builder's yard; dawn must be breaking.

Lara and Nik dropped into sleep like stones falling down a deep well.

They wakened stiff and cold. Their feet felt dead. A slight skim of frost covered the ground; the sky above was iron grey. They looked around them, frowning at the piles of old sacks, empty cement bags and rusted tools. Where were they?

Lara had been dreaming her burning dream again: she had seen flames leaping high, coloured red, orange, pink, purple, green. There seemed to have been people behind the flames but she could not see them. She awoke with a scream at the back of her throat. Nik's dream, too, had been luridly coloured; bodies had spun as if spiralling into outer space against a background of brilliant, strobing lights.

Gradually the remembrance of the night and its events came back to them. Their first concern was Oscar.

His head sagged sideways in the crook of Nik's arm, his limbs sprawled as if stuffed with straw. But he still breathed, though his colour had deteriorated even further and was now greyish, as if reflecting the sky overhead. They must make their way to Birch Street as soon as possible.

'One of us will have to go and find somebody to ask,' said Nik.

'I'll go.' Lara jumped up, wincing as pain jabbed her rib cage. She massaged it gently.

'Are you all right?'

'Fine.'

'It would be best if you went,' said Nik. Lara was better than he when it came to talking to people. She would be sure to find someone and engage them in conversation in no time at all.

'Take care!' he called after her. 'Watch out for police! Remember you have no papers!'

Lara peered into the street. It was deserted except for a scrawny cat that was nosing its way along the

gutter, looking for food, no doubt. When it saw
Lara it came and wound itself around her legs.

'Sorry, pussy, but I don't have any food, either.'
She scratched the back of its scabby neck with one
finger. It would probably have fleas. Poor animal.
Nothing but skin and bone. And a sore on one of its
back legs was oozing pus.

Lara realized she was hungry herself. Not just
hungry, but ravenous. It was hours since they had
eaten. And then it had been only a bowl of thin greasy
soup and a hunk of dry bread. In the last few days food
at the orphanage had been getting scarcer and scarcer.

Leaving the cat behind she continued along the
street. On the corner she came upon a road sweeper,
an old woman with her head bound up in a kerchief.
Lara wished her good morning, then asked if she
knew where Birch Street was.

'Never heard of it.'

Lara had sensed that the old woman was going to
say that. She had not repeated the name of the street
or even looked up. She had carried on sweeping with
her hard bristly broom, nudging her little dust-cart
in front of her. A lot of people were like that; they
didn't want to talk to you, didn't want to hear you,
didn't want to see you. They kept their heads down,
minded their own business. That way, they stayed
out of trouble. It didn't used to be like that, Biba
said. If you asked someone for help you would get
it. Living in a police state made people afraid of
their own shadows.

Lara walked on. She passed a few men going to
work; in their overalls and clumpy boots they looked
like factory workers. She was not sure about stop-

ping any of them. She, too, was suspicious of people.

Then she saw a young woman pushing a pram. This time she was lucky.

'Birch Street,' said the young woman, giving her a smile. 'Yes, I know it well. I have an aunt who lives nearby, on Linden Street.' She put the brake on the pram and came to the corner to give Lara directions.

Nik waited anxiously for Lara to return. He made Oscar as comfortable as he could, then he took a little exercise by walking up and down the yard. His legs were stiff. He stepped in and out and around the piles of rubbish.

In amongst the junk he found an old dust-cart. It had been covered with a cement sack; it was possible that someone had stolen it and had intended to come back for it later. Anything left lying around was liable to be stolen. The cart seemed in good enough working order. Nik spun the wheels in his hand.

Lara returned with the information that Birch Street was a good three kilometres away. 'How are we to carry Oscar that far? Especially when there are people about?'

'No problem.' Nik indicated the dust-cart. 'We've got a chariot!'

Getting Oscar into the cart was not easy, but after a struggle they succeeded. From time to time Oscar groaned and his eyes jerked open, though he did not appear to see them. The wound on his head was still seeping fresh blood and his brow felt feverishly hot.

His feet hung over the end of the cart.

'We'll have to cover him,' said Nik. 'Make it look as if we've only got junk.'

They heaped sacks on top of Oscar and draped his feet as best they could. Nik took off his anorak and arranged it over Oscar's head, leaving a vent so that he would be able to breathe.

Then Nik bent down and took hold of the handles of the cart.

MONDAY: *MORNING*

Their journey to Birch Street was to prove nerve-racking. Every time they heard a car engine they looked round. It was difficult not to. When they saw a police or army vehicle, their heartbeats quickened and their mouths dried. When the cars passed, they felt weak-kneed with relief.

Few of the people on the street gave them as much as a glance. They were used to odd sights. One woman at a street light asked, 'What have you got there? Anything to sell?' She poked the sacks with a long crooked finger. Lara thought it looked like a witch's finger. After their sojourn in the wood, she had witches on the brain! The woman's black hair hung in long greasy ropes down her back. 'You're hiding something,' she said with a laugh that sounded more like a cackle. 'I know you are.'

'They're only old sacks,' said Lara, whose eye was fixed firmly on the light, willing it to change.

'Could do with a sack or two. Sacks come in useful. For all sorts of things. You don't want all that lot, do you? You could spare me a sack, couldn't you?' wheedled the woman. She took hold of Lara's arm. Her fingers pinched the way Dracula's had.

Just then the light changed and the walking man came on. Lara and Nik stepped thankfully out into the road, and within seconds had outstripped the woman. If people thought you had anything that they didn't have they would follow you. The woman dogged their footsteps for a few metres and then dropped back.

Traffic was by now dense and a continuous stream of police cars and motor bikes was sweeping through the streets at alarming speeds, ignoring red lights and marked crossings, causing pedestrians to jump aside and cyclists to serve. The air reverberated with the clamour of sirens. Convoys of grey-green army trucks thundered past, crammed with soldiers. It seemed as if all the security forces in the country were on alert.

At one point Nik and Lara all but ran straight into the arms of a police foot-patrol. They caught sight of it just in time to dive into the mouth of an alley-way where they waited, squatting behind the dust-cart until the patrol had passed. They felt less nervous now, though; they were adjusting to the idea of danger.

The woman with the pram had given Lara good instructions. They found Birch Street without taking any wrong turnings. It proved to be a quiet cul-de-sac, backing on to a canal, well away from the main road and the sound of sirens. It was lined on either side by slender silvery birch trees. Up in the branches birds were singing, early migrants, returned from better climes, confident that soon the days and nights here would turn warmer. Whatever was going on in the world below did not seem to be disturbing them. They were soaring free, chirping vigorously, high above it all.

Number twenty-seven was an old, two-storeyed, semi-detached timbered house with a steeply sloping shingled roof. It was narrow-fronted, had one window up, and one down. Purple, white and yellow crocuses made brilliant spikes of colour in the little front garden, and by the hedge white narcissi bloomed.

Three steps took Lara and Nik up the short path to the front door, painted egg-yellow to match the crocuses. They knocked, then stood well back, so that Biba's sister would be able to observe them from the upstairs window if she wished. And they were fairly sure that she would wish. People did not open their doors to unexpected callers without first checking them out.

They had to knock a second time. Almost immediately the letter-box flap lifted and a muffled voice asked, 'Who is there?'

'Friends of Biba's,' Lara answered. 'From the orphanage. Biba gave us your address. And Oscar.'

'Oscar?'

'Biba's grandson. He is here, too. With us.'

The door opened then, and out on to the step came a little round dumpling of a woman, with eyes as black as currants. She was almost the double of Biba, only younger. Lara wanted to hug her.

Nina looked past them. A frown ridged her forehead below her dark blue kerchief. 'But where is Oscar?' she asked.

Nik lifted his anorak.

'My God!' shrieked Nina. 'He is dead!'

*

But Oscar still breathed, if shallowly. They carried him gingerly up the steep staircase to a first-floor bedroom and laid him in the middle of the large soft feather bed.

Nina threw on a shawl and went at once to fetch a doctor who lived nearby. A 'friendly' doctor. 'One of us,' she said. She returned with him.

After he'd examined Oscar he said that his head wound was fortunately superficial. Not that it was not serious, but a bullet had grazed it rather than entered the skull.

'Praise be to God!' Nina crossed herself.

'He's lost a lot of blood, though, and as you can see he's suffering from concussion. Rest, warmth and quiet – that's all I can prescribe. I have no medication I can give you, except for this handful of pain-killers. My stocks have almost run out. I take it you wouldn't want him to go to hospital?'

It was not a serious question. He knew as well as they that it would be dangerous for anyone with an unexplained gunshot wound to be admitted to hospital. Especially a student. Especially Oscar, who was known to the authorities as a dissident.

Nina said it had been announced on the news that morning that six students had been killed in the uprising and more than sixty arrested in different parts of the city. And many more were being sought. The Chief of Police had come on the radio to declare that he personally would stamp out the uprising until not even the tiniest spark survived. No quarter would be given to enemies of the state.

'The sparks won't be stamped out this time,' said the doctor as he sipped the tea prepared for him by

Nina. Nik and Lara drank, too, grateful for the hot reviving liquid. Precious tea. Nina must have been hoarding it for special occasions. 'The populace is alight!' said the doctor. 'They've had more than enough.'

'When I heard the news, I was worried sick about Oscar,' said Nina. 'I knew he'd be in the thick of it! That's the way he is. I thought of my poor sister Biba. How she loves that boy! The sun rises and sets on him for her.'

'I think you are rather fond of him yourself, Nina?' observed the doctor.

She smiled. 'That is true. And I shall take good care of him.'

'I'm sure you will.'

The doctor warned them that they must be extremely careful. A state of emergency had been declared and a night-time curfew was to come into force. No one other than security forces and people with permits were to be allowed on the streets between the hours of six in the evening and six in the morning. And all public demonstrations and gatherings had been banned.

After the doctor had gone, Nina set food on the table for Nik and Lara. They had black bread, pickled cucumbers and wafer-thin slices of salami. Nina had been out before dawn and queued for two hours for the meat.

'What about you?' asked Nik.

'I have eaten.'

'Are you sure?' Lara looked her in the eye.

'Eat! Do what Nina tells you! You need food. Two growing young people like you. Then you must sleep.'

They ate slowly, savouring the peppery taste of the salami, the sharp bite of the pickle and the solid comforting feel of the bread in their mouths. Nina watched them, nodding her head with approval. She had lit a small wood fire in the grate, which was crackling cheerfully at their backs. The room itself was comforting, with its rocking chair by the fire and scrubbed wood kitchen table and brightly coloured rag rug at their feet. And ranged around the walls were old framed photographs of Nina's family. They'd been peasant farmers. The pictures, turning brownish now from long exposure to the light, showed them ploughing and haymaking and bringing in the harvest.

'That's me!' Nina indicated a smiling young girl holding a pitchfork. 'And that's Biba. See how she's scowling! She had wanted to hold the pitchfork.' Nina laughed, at the memory of it.

When Lara and Nik had finished eating, Nina took them up the narrow flight of stairs to the top landing. There she set up a ladder.

'You see that trap door? Climb up, open it and go inside, then pull the ladder up behind you. And remember to close the trap door and secure the bolts. You'll find two straw palliasses and some old feather quilts. Up there you'll be safe, or as safe as it's possible to be.'

MONDAY: *AFTERNOON*

Nik and Lara slept for four hours and came back downstairs feeling refreshed.

Nina was in the kitchen ironing Oscar's white shirt. She had washed it and managed to bleach out the bloodstains. 'See – not a trace!' She held it against the light. 'He came round for a moment a little while ago and I'm sure he knew me. He tried to smile.'

'That's wonderful!' said Lara.

She froze as there came four staccato taps on the back door.

'It's all right, don't worry!' Nina set down the heavy flat iron. 'It'll be my neighbour Maria. That's our signal. We know it's safe to let one another in.'

Nina opened the door to admit a woman with rosy cheeks and white hair tied back in a bun. Nina introduced Nik and Lara.

'These are my young friends I told you about earlier who have come from Biba's orphanage.'

'Welcome to Birch Street!' said Maria, offering each of them her hand in turn.

She was carrying a parcel. 'This came yesterday from my relatives in Scotland, Nina. There are one or two things in it that might suit Lara and Nik.'

'Us!' exclaimed Lara.

'They are no use to me. My cousins always send some clothes for me to pass on to young people in the street.'

From the parcel Maria took a pair of blue jeans. She held them up. They'd been designed for someone long and skinny.

'They'd fit Nik,' said Biba, draping them against his legs. 'Perfect!'

Nik stammered out his thanks. He'd only ever had one pair of real jeans before and they'd been passed on to him when they'd been almost in tatters.

40

'And a sweatshirt,' said Maria.

It was sapphire-blue and had the letters SCOTLAND printed on it in white. That, too, fitted Nik. As did a pair of blue and white trainers that looked as if they'd been scarcely worn.

'You're in luck, boy!' said Nina. She glanced at Lara, who had gone quiet. 'I'm sure there'll be something for you, Lara.'

'Yes, I think there very well might well be.' Maria was rummaging again. 'What about these?' She brought out a pair of red velvet corduroy trousers.

'They're beautiful,' cried Lara. 'Do you mean I could really have them? To keep?'

'Yes, to keep. And this green sweatshirt would go nicely with them, don't you think? and what about these green and white trainers?'

The red trousers were a little long in the leg for Lara, but Nina quickly took them up. Her little fingers flew as they plied the needle. Before she'd retired she'd been a seamstress in a garment factory, had ended up as floor manageress. Now she lived on her state pension and by doing small sewing jobs for people in the neighbourhood.

Dressed in their new clothing, Lara and Nik paraded up and down the kitchen for the two women to inspect them.

'You look like millionaires,' declared Nina.

Lara laughed with delight. In these beautiful red trousers the colour of rosehips in autumn and this soft emerald green shirt she felt like a millionaire. She never wanted to wear the grey clothes of the orphanage again.

'Why do people in our country wear such drab clothes?' she asked.

'Probably because they don't dirty so quickly,' said Maria. 'After all, soap is scarce.'

'Perhaps people feel drab inside when they're repressed,' suggested Nina.

'You've got a bright yellow door!' said Lara.

Nina smiled.

Maria had something for Nina also. She produced two packets of stock cubes, one of chicken and the other beef, and a packet of Earl Grey tea.

'Earl Grey,' Lara read the words on the packet slowly. They had learnt a little English from the orphanage teacher. 'It sounds special, doesn't it?'

Nina sniffed it. 'Smells of bergamot. We'll try it later, shall we?'

In their excitement, they had forgotten Oscar. Nik said he would go up and sit with him.

He went straight away. First, he checked the street, then he pulled a chair close to the big bed. Oscar was tossing restlessly and muttering words that made no sense to Nik. Suddenly he quietened, and his eyelids flew upward.

His bright blue eyes stared questioningly at Nik.

'I'm Nik. From the orphanage.'

'Nik.' Oscar's lips framed the word.

Nik smiled and nodded. 'I'm here with Lara. You remember Lara – the dark girl with the wide brown eyes?'

'Yes. And Biba?'

'Biba is safe. She is at the orphanage with the children.'

'Good.'

Oscar closed his eyes again. It seemed to Nik that

his breathing was now more regular. He ran back downstairs to tell the others the good news.

TUESDAY: *MORNING*

By breakfast-time, Oscar had regained full consciousness. He was able to sit up and drink a cup of warm milk, precious milk that had been handed in by another neighbour whose son lived in the country. It was seldom that any could be found in the town. There was plenty of milk on the farms but no transport to bring it in.

Nina had sweetened the drink with honey.

'Honey,' Oscar murmured. 'Makes me think of summer. Where did you get it from, Nina?'

'Another neighbour, of course! He keeps bees.'

'You have good neighbours.'

'Good neighbours and good friends. Now that is enough talk from you! You're exhausting yourself.'

Oscar tried to insist that he felt perfectly fit. He pushed himself up from his pillows and flung back the covers. But when he made to get out of bed he found that the room went into a spin and he had to sit down.

'Now look at you!' scolded Nina. 'Weak as a newborn kitten. Back into bed with you! And stay there. The only answer is to tie you down.'

'I've got things to do, Nina. Urgent things.'

'I'm sure! I know what kind of things. You are not fit to be out and about.'

'But I *must* talk with my friends. To find out what's going on. We've got this network, and we have to keep passing information from one to the other.'

They brought the radio up to Oscar's room so that he could listen to the news bulletins.

'Not that they tell us the truth!' he said. 'We're given only the regime's version of it.' All radio and television stations were under the control of the government.

According to the news reports, the uprising was now dead, and all the troublemakers had been squashed. Oscar snorted, and moved restlessly in the bed.

Nina consoled him by telling him that different rumours were circulating in the food queues. She had heard there was still much unrest, and talk of plots and further uprisings. Up in the north of the country, the workers had gone on strike. Elsewhere, miners had downed tools. Fresh arrests were being made all the time, but in spite of that the protests and demonstrations were continuing.

'As soon as a dozen people gather together the police move in. They've closed the university. And the high schools. I've also heard it said that the army is getting ready to revolt.'

'Can it be true?' asked Nik. 'That the army would go against the state?'

'That's what they're saying.'

'It could well be true,' Oscar considered.

'They're men as well as soldiers, after all,' said Nina, echoing what the man in the square had said about the police. 'They've got mothers and fathers, sisters and brothers, wives and children. They're our countrymen. Why should they want to shoot us down?'

'Plenty do, Nina,' Oscar reminded her. 'The hard men are our countrymen too, let us not forget that!'

'Not true ones! They're evil men who only want power. I suppose every society has its evil men.'

'There are good people too, aren't there?' asked Lara anxiously. She was standing by the window, taking a turn to keep watch. They had to be vigilant and not forget for an instant that Oscar was a wanted man.

'Of course, Lara! You are right to remind us.' Nina pushed herself up from the low chair beside Oscar's bed. 'And now I must go and see to my soup. I managed to get some carrots and an onion today. So we are in luck! And I shall put in one of the chicken stock cubes that Maria gave me and a little pinch of tarragon from my garden. That will make it nice and tasty.'

'I'll come and help,' said Lara. 'I'll peel the vegetables.'

When the door had closed behind them, Oscar said, struggling to raise himself up against the pillows, 'Nik, could you come here a moment, please?'

Nik left the window to go to the bed.

'I've got something to ask you.' Oscar spoke hesitantly. 'A favour. I hate having to ask. I mean, you've already saved my life – you and Lara.'

Nik protested.

'Don't say it was nothing! To me it was everything!' Oscar tried to laugh, winced instead and touched his head.

'It still hurts?'

'Not too bad. I can't complain. Some of my friends won't have been as lucky. And that's what I'd like to ask you to do.'

'You want me to take a message to them?'

'Yes.' Oscar held up his hand. 'Don't answer straight away! Think about it. It could be dangerous. I'll understand if you say you'd prefer not to do it.'

TUESDAY: *3 p.m.*

Nik set out after lunch. This meant he would have three hours in which to deliver Oscar's message and return before the start of curfew at six o'clock.

'Take care!' Lara watched him go. She made a vivid splash of colour on the front step in her new red trousers and green sweater.

Nik was wearing his old clothes. Oscar had pointed out that people would pay less attention to him if he dressed in his usual colourless grey. They might glance curiously at the blue sweatshirt emblazoned with the letters SCOTLAND, and then look at his face, and remember him. The last thing Nik wanted on this outing was to be noticed and remembered.

He looked back from the corner to wave. He knew Lara would wait until he did. He saw her turn and go back into the house. Now he was on his own.

He was glad to be out and felt excited about his mission. It made him feel a part of what was going on. He was to take a message from Oscar to Stefan Bild, one of the main student leaders.

After a whole day in the house, he'd been feeling cooped up. He'd always found it difficult being boxed in by four walls. At the orphanage he had tried to work outside whenever possible; he had dug ditches, tilled the vegetable allotment, filled in the pot-holes in the drive, chopped wood.

46

He walked with a long easy stride, but didn't hurry. Don't look as if you're out on urgent business, Oscar had told him. It was important to look casual.

Police and army vehicles were still patrolling the main roads. Nik gave them only glancing looks and kept well away from the kerb-side of the pavement. He passed several long straggling queues of people waiting hopefully for the chance to buy a loaf of bread or a piece of meat. They paid no attention to him. They shuffled forward, keeping their eyes on the person in front, concerned that no one should push in and jump the queue. Queuing was part of everyday life. Only members of the armed forces were allowed to walk to the head of a queue.

Nik's mind was churning with the information Oscar had given him. Apparently, Stefan was holed up behind the top security jail, in a small apartment classed as a 'safe house'. It belonged to one of the warders at the jail who was sympathetic to their cause but who was thought by the authorities to be loyal to the regime. Remember, though, that no house is totally safe, Oscar had stressed. Nik was to approach the apartment warily and not reveal who he was until he was sure that the people inside were genuine. Oscar had rehearsed him through each stage, telling him, word for word, what he should say. And under no circumstances was he to diverge from the set piece.

Oscar had told him also exactly which route to take. He'd drawn a map, which afterwards he'd burnt. They had gone over and over it, until Nik had known by heart the names of the streets and on which corner he should turn right or left. Oscar had cross-questioned him. 'When you reach the Markets, which way do you go?' 'Turn left into Fishmonger's Lane, then right into Silversmith Street.' Nik must on no account appear to be *looking* for an address. He must walk in the way that someone who was familiar with the city would. He must not hesitate on corners or stop to read street names. And if he should be stopped by police he was to say he was living with his Aunt Nina on Birch Street and that she had sent him out to look for milk. Nina had given him a few coins to help make his story credible. He jingled them in his pocket as he walked.

He reached the Markets. The stalls were bare and unattended. Rotting vegetable leaves speckled the ground, broken boxes lay scattered at random, pigeons pecked in amongst the waste. Also scavenging were two old men who pounced with mittened hands on anything that looked semi-edible.

On arriving at Fishmonger's Lane Nik turned left without having to think and continued towards the city centre. It all seemed terribly easy so far. No one was showing the least bit of interest in him. He came to Cathedral Square, saw that it was barricaded off by tanks whose turrets bristled with guns. Soldiers lounged around, some leaning against the walls of their tanks with their arms folded and their caps tipped backward on their foreheads. They looked bored. A smell of burning lingered in the air.

Nik skirted the square, and came to the prison. His throat swelled as he allowed himself a quick glance at the high grim wall. His father had hated walls too; he'd been a man who had loved the out-of-doors. They used to go fishing together, and bird-watching. They'd camp up north, in the mountains, amongst the tall pine trees, and wake in the morning to see the first streaks of colour come seeping into the eastern sky. Then they'd wash in a cool, rushing mountain stream. It had been peaceful there.

Nik left the wall behind. He turned right, then left, and left again. He was in the right street, had reached his objective. It was a street of grey stone tenement buildings, four storeys high. There was no one about. It was eerie how many streets were deserted, whereas the main roads bustled with the activity of the security forces.

He crossed the road. A few steps took him to number eleven. He looked right and left, then pushed open the bottom door, which stood ajar, and entered a dark hallway. As his eyes grew accustomed to the change of light he saw the curve of a narrow staircase with a black iron railing leading upward. He climbed the first flight, met no one, went up the next.

The apartment should be on this floor. As he'd come higher he'd been able to see more clearly; a skylight was letting in a little watery sunlight. The stair smelt sour, of cats and cooking odours and stinking lavatories. Large parts of the city smelt this way.

He identified the door. The first on the left facing the top of the stairs. The door had no colour; any paint that had ever adorned it had long since worn off. It bore no name, nor number, either. All this was as it should be, as he had been told he would

49

find it. Everything appeared to be going according to plan. Why then should he feel so nervous now?

He could hear no sound other than that of a steady drip, drip, drip of water coming from somewhere on the outside of the building. A leaking downpipe, more than likely. It was the quiet that was making him feel uneasy. The back of his neck prickled. He felt he was being watched.

He shook himself. He couldn't be. There were no peep-holes in the other doors, only in this one, and he was standing well to the side of it.

He stepped now into the sight range of the peep-hole, as Oscar had instructed; the door would not be opened otherwise. He would have to be seen. Taking a deep breath to calm himself, he raised his knuckles and rapped twice in rapid succession, paused, and rapped again.

For a good minute, nothing happened. It was a long minute. He counted the seconds in his head, felt them beating like a metronome inside his skull. Tick, tock. His mother had taught piano. He remembered her long slender fingers as they set the metronome going. And her smile when she looked up. Sweat was starting around his hairline. He wiped his forehead with the back of his arm.

He heard footsteps. Slow and deliberate. Not hurrying at all. They stopped. He sensed an eye, narrowed, beamed straight at him, through the tiny glass hole in the door. He swallowed to ease the tension in his throat and took a step backward.

The door opened and a man in a crumpled navy-blue suit appeared in the doorway. At once alarm signals rang in Nik's head.

50

TUESDAY: *4 p.m.*

The man facing Nik did not fit Oscar's description
of the warder, who should be stockily built and
almost completely bald, except for a monk-like fringe
of black hair. The man in the doorway was round-
shouldered, had a narrow face and a shock of ginger
hair with a spidery moustache to match. Nor did he
look like a student. He was too old for that. His
mouth was thin, and there was something mean
looking about it. Nik began to feel deeply uneasy.

'Are you looking for someone?' asked the man.

'Peter Frank.'

'Peter Frank, eh?'

'Yes.'

'What do you want with him?'

That was not the right response. The man should
have said: 'I've never heard of him!' Of course he
could have recently taken refuge in this house himself
and not known the codes. But Nik did not believe
that, and hadn't Oscar said not to deviate at all
from the routine? And the man had not opened the
door on a chain in the first instance, which he
should have done. Something must have gone
wrong.

Perhaps Stefan had been arrested! Perhaps the
warder had not been on their side after all. He might
have been a double agent. A spy set in the midst of
the student camp. Or else he, too, had been taken
away. This man with the ginger hair could easily be
from the security services. His suit seemed to suggest
that. As did the way he was standing in the doorway,

regarding Nik. Like a cat eyeing its prey. Nik prepared himself for flight.

The man repeated, 'So what do you want with Peter Frank, lad?'

'His Aunt Helga is ill. I have been sent to fetch him.'

'So his aunt is ill, eh?'

'Yes.'

'I hope it's not serious?' The man seemed to be mocking him. He leant his shoulder against the jamb of the door and eased a squashed packet of cigarettes from his hip pocket. He shook out a cigarette and placed it between his pallid lips. When he had lit it he tossed the spent match at Nik's feet. It seemed to Nik like a challenge. The man blew out a long stream of smoke, keeping his eyes all the while on Nik's face. 'So, is she at death's door, Aunt Helga, would you say?'

'She has bad bronchitis.'

'Bronchitis?'

'Yes.'

'That's nasty. Who is this Peter Frank, then?' The man's tone changed. His voice became brisk and businesslike. He pushed himself up from the door jamb and took a step closer to confront Nik. 'Is he a student?'

'No, I don't think so,' said Nik quickly. 'I don't know him myself. His aunt asked me to come for him. But it seems that he isn't here?' He was aware he was talking much too fast and the man was registering that. He began to inch away. He could smell the man's smoky breath on his face.

'I haven't said that, have I? Why don't you come

inside and we'll discuss it? Someone else here might know this Peter Frank.'

'No, it's all right, thank you. I don't want to bother you.'

'No bother. You seem in a hurry, my young friend?'

'No, I mean, yes. Well, it's just that I have to find him, you see. His aunt is quite ill.' Nik's hand groped and found the banister rail. At the same time he let his right foot slide down a step. Should he cut and run? But that would give the game away completely. Try not to run if you can avoid it, Oscar had said.

A door opening on the landing above caused a small distraction. The man looked up and Nik took the opportunity to begin his retreat.

'Hey, come back here! Who are you? What's your name? Come back! I want to talk to you, young fellow!'

Nik fled, leaping down two, three steps at a time. He reached the first landing. He heard a number of voices shouting overhead, ordering him to come back. He went crashing down the second flight, pushed open the door and was out in the street within seconds.

He ran, as if he had a wind behind him. Even this contingency had been taken care of. Continue along the street, Oscar had instructed him, take the second left and first right and there you will find an old disused bakery. Go round to the back and crawl inside the ruined outhouse.

It was there, just as Oscar had said. Nik crept into the outhouse and flopped down on the floor. His heart was leaping about as if demented. He had left the man in the navy-blue suit well behind, he was fairly confident about that. The man had not moved fast enough. His body had looked slack and not very fit.

When he had recovered, Nik sat cross-legged on the stone-flagged floor, with his elbows resting on his knees and his chin cupped between his hands. Lara called it his thinking pose. He didn't have all that many thoughts at that moment, he was too intent on listening. His ears registered every tiny sound, then gradually he began to relax.

Time passed, but he could not tell how much. Once he'd had a watch, when he was small, four or five years old. It'd had a Mickey Mouse face on the dial and a red strap. He'd been very proud of that watch, had enjoyed being able to tell his friends the time. A cousin in America had sent it to him. From a place called Albuquerque. That was in New Mexico. He hadn't been sure how to pronounce it. He'd looked it up on the map with his father and he'd imagined the watch coming all the way across the North American continent and the Atlantic Ocean, and then Europe, to him. When the watch stopped after a few months, they had been unable to buy batteries to replace the dead ones.

Don't leave your hiding place for some considerable time, Oscar had said. Wait at least an hour and then come out cautiously, look all around and proceed only when you see that the coast is clear.

An hour. Nik reckoned he had been there for fifteen, or at the most, twenty minutes. He dozed.

*

Coming round he stretched as best he could in the limited space. His arms and legs felt tight and cramped. The roof was low over his head; reaching up he could touch it. He wondered if an hour or more had passed, but when he crawled to the doorway and peered out he saw that darkness had crept in amongst the buildings round about.

Looking up he saw there was a little more light left in the sky. He was aware, though, that it must be well past curfew-time.

TUESDAY: *4.30 p.m.*

Lara could not sit still. She paced between the bed and the window, stopping from time to time to look down into the street. Nothing much was happening there. A woman with a small child went by. He was crying and plucking at his mother's skirt, asking to be picked up. Lara thought with a pang of little Katya who, she knew, would be missing her. Two women wearing head scarves had passed earlier, carrying shopping bags. Now she saw them return, their bags as flat and empty-looking as when they had set out.

In the big, soft feather bed, Oscar slept on his back, his arms sprawled above his head. He had bursts of energy during which he would talk and talk and then, after a while, they could see the steam fizzling out of him and he would collapse, like a punctured tyre. Nina would cluck and scold and make him lie back against the pillows.

She came in, bearing mugs of camomile tea. 'We'll

55

let him sleep.' She nodded towards Oscar. 'He needs rest more than anything.'

She and Lara drew up chairs to the window. Lara glanced at her watch.

'It's a quarter to five. It's starting to get dark out, don't you think?'

'It's just that the sun has gone in, and the sky is overcast. It'll be light for a good while yet.'

'Only an hour and a bit till curfew.'

'He'll be back, don't worry! He's probably stopped a while with the students.'

They drank their tea and then Nina went back downstairs to make their supper.

Lara remained by the window, watching the street darken. Dusk stole in amongst the chimney pots. The street lights flickered, and some came on. It was seldom that all the lights worked at once. Men and women began to come home from work. Some walked alone, others were in groups of two or three, talking earnestly, heads bent. Sometimes they glanced over their shoulders. They were not talking about trivial things like the weather or the state of their gardens, you could tell that.

Nik was not amongst them.

Oscar stirred, and Lara went to him.

'Nik?' he asked, rubbing his eyes.

'He's not back yet.'

Oscar frowned and sat up. He swung his legs over the side of the bed. 'It's time for me to get up. I can't lie here like an invalid any longer! There's too much to be done.'

Lara left him and ran down to the kitchen. 'Nina, Oscar's getting up.'

'I knew I wouldn't be able to keep him tied down much longer!'

The hands of the kitchen clock stood at a quarter to six.

'It's a minute or two fast,' said Nina.

'But only a minute or two.'

Lara went to the front door, and opening it looked out into the street. It was empty now. Everyone seemed to be home who was coming. There were lights in most of the windows and glimmering blue rectangles marked out the houses that were fortunate enough to own television sets.

She walked along to the corner, hugging her arms across her chest to keep warm. A cool, skittish breeze had sprung up and she had not stopped to put on her anorak. She decided to go as far as the next corner where she would be able to see up to the main road. Come quickly, Nik! she pleaded inside her head. Don't get caught in the curfew! *Please don't!*

The beam of car lights coming towards her made her jump back. She didn't know whether to stand her ground or run. Oscar had warned them about running. Under almost any circumstances, he'd said. It would make you look as if you were up to something suspicious. If someone was chasing you, then that of course would be a different matter.

Lara stayed where she was, trying to look unconcerned. But when the car drew closer, she saw that it had a red light on its roof. And on its side the word POLICE was marked in large white letters. She was unable to staunch the shiver of fear that made her neck twitch.

The car pulled into the kerb alongside her, and a policeman put his head out of the window.

'What are you doing standing there, young lady?'

'Nothing.'

'Are you waiting for someone?'

'No. Nobody. Nobody at all.' She shouldn't go on, she knew that. It would only make her sound guilty. But knowing things didn't mean that you could always carry them out. 'I was just going,' she added lamely.

'It's five minutes to six! You must know there's a curfew in force?'

'Oh yes, yes of course.'

'Well, then?'

'I didn't realize . . .' She had been about to say she didn't have a watch. Hurriedly she put her hands behind her back.

The policeman kept his eyes on her face. 'Where do you live?' he asked.

'Birch Street.'

'I know Birch Street. I have a relative who lives on Birch Street. At number thirteen. What number are you?'

'Twenty-seven.'

'Do you live there with your parents?'

'No, with my Aunt Nina.'

'Get going then!'

She went, trying to restrain her legs. Walk, don't run! she told herself. When the car lights had swept on by and the street was returned to its state of semi-darkness, she broke into a trot. She wished she hadn't had to tell him where she was living. And the number, too! Especially when he had a relative in

the street who might be able to tell him that Nina
had no nieces. She hadn't thought fast enough. She
should have said she lived on Linden Street. But
then he might have insisted on taking her there.
'Jump in!' he might have said, and opened the black
car door.

What if he were to come to Nina's house? What if
he were to come, and find Oscar?

TUESDAY: *6 p.m.*

It was striking six as Lara came into the house.
Oscar and Nina were sitting at the kitchen table with
the radio placed between them.

Oscar looked up at Lara.

'There's no sign of Nik. But a police car stopped
me and the driver asked what I was doing. I had to
tell him where I lived. I didn't know what else to do.'

'Sit down, child,' said Nina. 'And don't worry! Of
course you had to say where you lived. One should
try not to lie unless one absolutely has to. Lies are
too easily found out.' She shook her head. 'Do you
hear what I've just said to you? Once upon a time I
would have told you not to lie because it was
wrong!'

Oscar put a finger to his lips. The news was about
to start. Lara joined them at the table. They sat with
their heads close to the radio, anxious not to miss a
word. The message was the same as usual: the government was continuing to keep a firm hold on the
country and the city had been fully restored to its
former peaceful state.

'Peaceful!' snorted Oscar. 'Fearful, more like.'

'An important arrest was made this afternoon,' the bulletin continued. 'The student dissident leader, Stefan Bild, along with a number of his fellow troublemakers, was apprehended at an apartment near the top security prison. Taken into custody at the same time was a warder from the prison who had been giving them sanctuary.'

'*Arrested!*' said Oscar, when he was able to speak. He looked stunned. 'This is terrible news!'

'Nik?' whispered Lara.

'He might not have got there before they were arrested,' said Nina, though she looked as worried as Lara felt.

'But he could have walked straight into their arms!' Oscar sprang up. 'I should never have asked him to go. He's just a kid. I've got to do something!'

'What can you do?' asked Nina. 'If you go out you'll be seen by the police. They'll be on the streets in force, you can be sure of that. It wouldn't help Nik if you were to get arrested as well.'

'I suppose not.' Oscar slumped back down onto his chair. He gave a long sigh and for a moment covered his face with his hands. During that moment Lara felt despair chilling her heart.

They listened to the rest of the news in silence. It was nothing but government propaganda. Everything was fine now, everyone was happy with their lot, the unrest had been caused by only a handful of troublemakers. Discontents. Riff-raff whom society could do without. This morning, the President had visited a hospital in the city and received a rapturous welcome from staff and patients alike. They heard the cheers on the radio. They heard people shouting, '*Long live –* '

Oscar snapped off the radio in disgust.

'Lies! Fabrications! It's so easy to bear false witness. Meanwhile we have to sit here like dummies!' Oscar slammed the table with his fist.

'Let us have some soup,' said Nina, rising to go to the stove. 'That will warm us.' And console us, Lara knew she meant. Whenever they hit a low spot, Nina would produce soup or camomile tea.

Lara drank her soup, even though she had no appetite, and after the first spoonful, found that the warm liquid was indeed soothing. Nina did not need to remind them to keep their strength up. Her eyes, fixed on them, said it all. If your belly was empty the world was more difficult to cope with. That was what Biba used to tell them too. You can't do anything if you're racked with hunger pains.

Lara thought of Biba and little Katya and wished that she and Nik were back with them now, in the orphanage. It was strange how, when they were there, they had hated the place and talked endlessly about escape. They had dreamed about it. But now that they had left, the big ugly building seemed like a place of refuge.

Where *was* Nik? Lara felt sick at the thought of him being out in the pitch-dark night alone, or locked up in some stinking little cell, which would be even worse. They might torture him, to get information. Information about Oscar. They must know that Oscar was Biba's grandson and it wouldn't take long for them to find out that Nik had come from the orphanage.

'Don't let your soup get cold!' Nina chided.

As Lara took up her spoon again, there came a loud knock on the front door. She dropped the spoon, spilling soup down her chin.

'Nik!' She leapt up.

'Wait!' cautioned Oscar. 'Don't open the door until we find out who it is.'

'Oscar's right,' said Nina.

He went first into the dark hall, with Nina and Lara following close behind. They moved quietly, like cat burglars. Oscar held up his hand to Nina, who nodded, understanding that she should wait there. Oscar and Lara dashed up the stairs.

The knock came again, a heavy knock; and to their anxious ears it sounded impatient. Nik would not knock in that way, unless perhaps he was in a panic. But surely then he would call out and say his name.

Oscar and Lara went into the front bedroom and crossed to the window to look down.

Outside in the street, parked at the kerb in front of the house, stood a police patrol car.

TUESDAY: *9 p.m.*

Nik disturbed a small stone underneath his foot when he tried to make a move. In his ears it made a noise like a boulder being hurled from a high cliff. Idiot! Silently he cursed himself. He stood so still he was almost quivering, and listened to the rasping sound of his own breathing. Even that sounded loud.

After a moment, he started again in the direction of the doorway. He knew it would be more sensible to stay under cover while the curfew was on but he couldn't bear the idea of spending the night in the outhouse. Somehow or other he was going to have to get back to Nina's. He knew they would be anxious about him. Oscar might even come looking for him. And if anyone should stay off the streets at present it was Oscar.

Nik emerged from the outhouse into the yard. Moonlight raked it, revealing deep violet shadows close to the walls. In front of him was the bakehouse itself, a low stone building with a broken gable-end. Half the city was broken. No one had money or materials to repair anything.

Then he heard a noise coming from inside the bakehouse. Someone had sneezed!

Nik felt as if the hairs on the back of his neck were standing on end, like a dog's, when danger is in the offing. There was someone on the other side of the wall. He flattened himself against it, afraid to move either forwards or back. The sneeze had been a quiet one, cut off midway, but he was sure he had heard it.

From the distance came the steady roar of traffic, punctuated at intervals by the high, blood-curdling wail of sirens. Here in the yard it was suffocatingly quiet.

Now he thought he heard a footstep. Or was he just imagining it? When you were on edge, it was easy to imagine anything. But no, someone – or something – *was* stirring on the other side of the wall.

Human or animal? Friend or foe?

Nik braced his body, ready for flight.

There came the sound of another footstep, quiet and tentative, as if testing the ground. Nik had an agonising cramp in his own left foot. He shifted it, only a fraction, but he *heard* it. And so, too, must have done the other person, for it was then that he spoke.

'Who is there?' a voice asked softly.

Nik did not answer.

A shadow appeared in the doorway of the bakehouse. Nik made out the dark shape of a man, of above medium height and broad build. His hair touched his collar. Nik could see nothing of his face.

'I'm a friend,' said the shadow.

'How do I know?'

'I'm a friend of Stefan's.'

'Stefan?'

'Yes, Stefan Bild.'

Nik let out a sigh of relief and stepped forward. The shadow came forward, too, and Nik saw that he looked like a student, of about Oscar's age, perhaps a little older. He was dressed in jeans, patched on one knee, and a dark reefer jacket.

'I'm Max. What do they call you?'

'Nik.'

'Pleased to meet you, Nik.' Max extended his hand, and after a slight hesitation, Nik took it. 'It's curfew time now, but I expect you know that?'

Nik nodded. 'Yes, I got caught out. That was why I came here to hide.'

'Me too. I went to visit Stefan and found he'd already had some visitors.'

'That's what happened to me!'

'Yes, the pigs had got there first! How do you come to know Stefan?'

'I don't really know him. I was taking a message.'

'Ah, from whom? Anyone I know?'

'Oscar?'

'Oscar Lind?'

'Yes! I suppose you would know him since he's a friend of Stefan Bild's.'

'Ours is a small world.'

Nik presumed that Max was also here in the outhouse because it was on a list of the network's refuges.

Max took a cigarette from his pocket and lit it. He cupped his hands to shelter the match and when Nik saw his mouth in the flare of light he began to wonder if he should have told him about Oscar. It looked a tight, rather pinched mouth. It reminded him of the mouth of the ginger-haired man. How stupid he was being! How could he judge someone's mouth, seen for less than half a minute, bunched up round a cigarette? But a little niggle of worry had started to torment him. Biba used to say you could read a person's character on their face.

Now that Nik had time to reflect, he knew he'd been wrong to blurt out Oscar's name so readily. He should have tried first to make sure that he could trust Max.

'Where are you going now, Nik?'

'I don't know.'

'Where do you live?'

'The other side of town, beyond the Markets area.'

'Can I come with you? I have nowhere to go. The police have taken over my apartment. I was hoping to find shelter with Stefan. And I want to make contact with Oscar, especially now that Stefan has been arrested.'

'What about the curfew?'

'We can manage that if we're careful. I'm used to moving about the city without being seen. Shall we go?'

Max led the way. He peered out into the street, then summoned Nik to follow. They proceeded in fits and starts, flitting from shadow to shadow, crouching behind walls, concealing themselves in doorways. Max moved with confidence. He seemed to be able to detect trouble up ahead, like an animal sniffing a scent in the wind. They lay low while foot patrols passed, then slunk out to cover a few more metres. Max obviously knew the city thoroughly. He led them down side streets and up back alleys, over high walls and across deserted yards. Cats streaked away in front of them. Rats scuttled. A dog set up a high, anxious barking but was quietened by a few words from Max.

They rested for a moment in an alley-way and Max lit another cigarette.

'Bad habit, eh, Nik?'

Nik shrugged.

'It helps calm the nerves, or so I tell myself. What's the name of your street, by the way? Where is it that we're making for exactly?' Max had asked in a casual sort of way, but underneath Nik thought the questions seemed insistent.

'Larch Street,' he said.

The lie had come out without his consciously considering it. He *thought* Max was probably all right, but he could not be totally sure. *Be cautious*, Oscar had impressed on him over and over again, until Nik had found himself becoming rattled. He'd thought Oscar had been going on too much. 'Okay, I hear you,' he'd wanted to say. 'I've got the message.' Now he was rattled with himself for having thrown caution to the winds. He'd been so relieved when the shadow had turned out to be not a policeman that he'd forgotten Oscar's warning.

What if Max was a member of the Secret Police? How could he find out? Then he remembered the passwords. Why hadn't he thought of them earlier? The cold in the outhouse must have penetrated his brain.

'Do you know Peter Frank?' asked Nik.

'Peter Frank? Yes, I'm sure I do. Name rings a bell. He's a friend of Oscar's, isn't he?'

He should have said he had never heard of him.

'He has a sister Hilda,' said Nik.

'Ah, yes, Hilda! I know Hilda. Nice girl.'

He should have said now that name rings a bell and he thinks he might have met her at a party, with her sister Lena.

Nik decided to try another sequence that Oscar had taught him.

He cocked his head as if he were listening. 'Sounds like the wind is rising.'

'Do you think so? I hadn't noticed.'

He should have said, 'It always does at night.'

'It will fan the fires,' said Nik.

'Most have been put out,' said Max.

He should have said, 'Night fires burn brightest.'

67

TUESDAY: *7 p.m.*

Nina opened the door to find a policeman standing on the step.

'I saw a girl,' he said. 'Down there, on the corner, one street over. She said she lived here?'

'That would be my niece Lara.'

The policeman glanced past Nina into the hallway.

Nina went to the foot of the stairs. 'Lara!' she called.

After a moment Lara appeared at the top of the stairs.

'Come down, child,' said Nina. 'There is someone here who wants to speak to you.'

Lara came slowly down the stairs. Her heart was bumping around, yet she felt herself to be perfectly calm on the surface. She knew, though, that her cheeks must look hot. She allowed a hand to stray up and pass lightly over one, then she smoothed a wandering lock of hair back behind her ear, trying to appear unperturbed.

'Ah, there you are!' said the policeman. 'I just wanted to be sure you'd got home safely. The streets aren't safe places to be out on these days, especially after dark. I have a young daughter myself.'

'You do?' said Nina.

'Must be about the same age as young Lara here.' He seemed in no hurry to go. He told them his daughter's name was Marta and that she was a wonderful gymnast. 'She was noticed when she was only five years old, picked out of her class at

68

school. She hopes to compete in the next Olympic Games.'

'You must be proud of her,' said Nina.

'Do you like gymnastics, Lara?' he asked.

'I haven't done very much.'

To Nina he said, 'You wouldn't have some tea by any chance, mistress?'

'I do, a little,' answered Nina. It was not possible to refuse a policeman's request. 'Would you care for a cup?'

'I would, very much. My throat is parched. I've been on duty all day. And now I'm to be on all night. It's this state of emergency!' He came in smartly, closed the door behind him and took off his cap.

Lara glanced with dismay at Nina, whose face remained smooth and impassive beneath its dark blue kerchief. What if Nik were to return now? He'd see the police car outside of course, and not come in. But he'd be bound to feel a little panicked and think that the police had come to arrest Oscar. And perhaps that *was* why this man was here. He seemed friendly enough and straightforward, like any ordinary man, but how could you tell if he was genuine or not? All this talk about his daughter might be just to make them relax. They could be crafty, the people who worked for the security forces. They didn't always come barging in with their boots clumping and their voices bouncing off the walls.

And then there was Oscar, who by now would be up in the loft with his ear pressed against the trap door, trying to make out what was going on. Lara hoped he wouldn't think that the closing of the door meant the policeman had gone. But he was too experienced to presume that. He would wait until she came up to tell him the coast was clear.

They went into the kitchen and the policeman settled himself in the big rocker beside the empty grate. They had little wood left, so Nina had decided to wait until eight o'clock before lighting the fire. The policeman sighed as if it were a relief to be off duty for a few minutes. He unbuttoned his jacket and rocked gently to and fro.

Lara suddenly registered the three mugs sitting on the table right in front of his nose. *Three* mugs.

'Do you two live on your own here together?'

'We do.' Nina ran water into the kettle.

Lara sidled round the edge of the table, and while the man's eyes were on Nina she seized one of the three mugs. Keeping her back to him she went over to the window and laid it gently in the sink. When Nina had finished filling the kettle, Lara rinsed the mug under the tap, then quickly dried it with the cloth hanging over the end of the draining board. Their self-invited guest seemed not to have noticed. He was watching Nina light the gas and asking her if she was able to get fuel.

'Not much.'

'These are hard times.' He looked at Lara. 'Those are nice clothes that you've got on.'

'My neighbour gave them to her,' said Nina. 'She got a parcel from abroad.'

'Ah, she has relatives in the west then, your neighbour?'

To Lara's ears every question that he asked sounded loaded.

He slid his hand into his shirt pocket. 'Would you like to see a photograph of my daughter Marta?'

Nina and Lara put their heads together to look at the picture.

'She looks a fine girl,' commented Nina.

The girl was wearing a black leotard and was standing poised on a barre on one foot.

'Very nice,' murmured Lara.

It was impossible to tell if the girl was nice or nasty. She was staring straight ahead with a wooden expression on her face. Concentrating on not falling off, no doubt. Or perhaps she was bored rigid. Biba said that child athletes and dancers who were chosen young had to work terribly hard. They often had to practise for as much as ten hours a day. They were expected to win international competitions and bring glory to the country. Biba thought it was not a good life for them. They burned out early and had no time to be children. Lara and some of the other girls at the orphanage used to dream of being chosen. They would walk along fallen tree trunks in the overgrown garden, balancing, with their arms waving up and down like aeroplane wings, pretending to be ballet dancers.

'She must be very agile,' Nina commented.

'Like a cat. She is good at all sports. What about you, Lara? What do you like to play?'

'Basketball.' They had played a few times at the orphanage, but they'd never had much time for sports. The Crow said they could exercise themselves by working and making themselves useful. Sometimes, when he and Dracula went off on a week-end trip, they would bring out an old ball and have a game of football. That had been fun.

'I think you would be good at basketball. You have long arms. Your school should encourage you.'

Please let him drop the subject, she prayed. Please don't let him ask me what school I go to. For then the fat would be in the fire and he would ask what she was doing here and why she was not at the orphanage.

Nina intervened. 'Are you from the city yourself?' she asked their visitor.

'No, I come from a small village a hundred kilometres to the south.' He began to reminisce, to tell them about the little school he had gone to and how he had worked on a local farm in summer-time, herding cows in his bare feet. 'We used to warm our feet in the cow pats! I'm not sure now why I left my village to come into the town. To make my fortune, I suppose! I'd have done better to stay.'

Nina poured the tea. They each had a cup with a spoonful of runny raspberry jam stirred in for sweetness. Lara slipped hers slowly, enjoying the warm liquid as it slid down her dry throat. He did seem to be all right, this man. Perhaps he just wanted a little time away from his job. To be off-duty. It couldn't be a very nice job, after all, rounding up people and dragging them off to prison. Not unless you were a pretty nasty person. He didn't look nasty. He had a ruddy, open, countryish sort of face and round blue eyes. Perhaps he'd become a policeman because there wasn't anything else for him to do. He might even have been drafted into the force. He could have gone to his relative's house, though, couldn't he, if he'd simply wanted some time off? Though Nina had said that the woman in number thirteen was elderly, and stone deaf. Lara's head buzzed with thoughts.

Their visitor was looking more relaxed by the minute, as he sprawled in the chair with his jacket open. He was enjoying telling them about his childhood and now Nina was joining in with tales about hers. Her parents had kept goats, a few hens and a cow on their small parcel of land.

'We grew most of our own food. We had everything we needed.'

'Those were the days!'

Nina did not comment on that, for even to agree might be taken as a criticism of the regime which ruled them now. She asked if he would like more tea.

'Is there any?'

'I think I can squeeze out another half cup.'

'You are kind, mistress. If I come by some eggs or a bit of bacon I'll remember you.'

'I would appreciate that.'

It was well known that members of the security forces could get extra food. People gave it to them, as bribes, to keep in with them.

The policeman stayed for an hour. Eventually he got up, yawning, saying he supposed he'd better move along. Taking his time, he buttoned up his jacket, then he lifted his cap from the table. Nina and Lara accompanied him out to the hall.

He paused at the foot of the stairs to glance up. 'It's a good house you have.'

'Yes,' agreed Nina, her hand resting on the door knob, ready to turn it and pull it open.

'You have plenty of room?'

'Two bedrooms.'

He looked now at the other door off the hall, which stood closed.

'That's my parlour. I use it in summer-time only. In winter it's too cold. It faces north.' Nina threw open the door and switched on the light as if to show that she had nothing to hide.

She was right about the lack of heat; a blast of chill air struck them as the door swung inward. The policeman took a step inside the room. It was furnished with two over-stuffed armchairs in faded yellow brocade, raggedy thin on the backs and arms, and a sofa to match, and a big old mahogany sideboard on which sat two heavy brass candlesticks. The furniture filled the little parlour. On the back wall hung a carved wooden cross. If he noticed the cross, he did not remark on it. It was forbidden to display religious symbols.

'You're lucky to have so much space for the two of you.'

'I had three lodgers until last week. They had to move away, up north, for work.'

'We're tight for space in our house. My Marta has to share with her three brothers. She's always grumbling about that! My old father lives with us, too. He shares a bedroom with my wife and myself. The housing shortage is bad.' He glanced up the stairs again. 'Have you an attic as well?'

Lara held her breath.

'Only a loft.' Nina's voice remained calm. 'We use it for storage.'

'Ah, well, I'll bid you both good night.' He set his cap on his head. 'And thank you again, mistress, for your kind hospitality.'

'You're welcome.'

Nina opened the door and he stepped out.

'Good night!' they called after him.

They watched until he got into his car, then Nina closed the door.

'Thank goodness!' said Lara. 'I thought he would never go. I thought he was going to suggest putting a lodger in with us. I suppose he still could?'

'Yes, he could.'

'I thought he was probably all right, though?'

'Yes, probably.'

'But you're not sure?'

'One can seldom be absolutely sure, Lara. Sadly.'

The evening dragged.

'He *must* have run into the police,' said Lara for the umpteenth time. And here they were sitting drinking camomile tea and doing nothing about it! Worse than that was the knowledge that there was nothing they could do, even after the curfew would be lifted at dawn.

'We'd best go to bed,' said Nina, rising, cutting off the conversation. She lifted the mugs from the table.

'*Bed?*' said Lara.

'We can't sit here all night. He won't come now. We need our rest.'

'Nina's right.' Oscar pushed back his chair and stood up. 'If we can get some sleep we'll be able to think more clearly tomorrow.' He touched Lara's shoulder. 'I'm sorry, Lara.'

'It's not your fault,' she said gruffly, though she couldn't help feeling it was, at least partly. He shouldn't have sent Nik with the message. Nik was too young to be sent on dangerous missions. He had only just turned thirteen, after all. But she knew that Nik had desperately wanted to go and he'd been annoyed with her when she'd suggested that maybe he shouldn't.

Nina put out the lights and they went upstairs. Lara might as well sleep in the spare bedroom, said Nina, now that the policeman knew she lived here. There was little point in her trying to hide. Oscar climbed on up to the attic.

Lara went reluctantly to bed. She took a last look into the street, but nothing was moving. She thought she would lie awake all night, but within seconds she had dropped into a deep sleep.

TUESDAY: *11 p.m.*

Nik and Max were crouched in a motor mechanic's yard, behind an old rusted car. Its door was hanging off and its wheels had been removed. Vandals had been inside too, had torn apart the upholstery and pulled out the innards. They'd taken everything that could be unscrewed or unhinged, from the steering wheel to door handles. Something moved inside the chassis. A rat, probably.

'Those damned rats are everywhere,' said Max. 'The city's rotten with them. We need to exterminate them.' He seemed to be speaking to himself more than to Nik.

On the other side of the garage forecourt the street swarmed with dark-uniformed policemen. Several cars had come screeching round the corner with their red lights whirling on their roofs and their klaxons blaring, sending Nik and Max diving for cover. The police had kicked in the door of a warehouse across the street and half a dozen of them had entered the building in a rush.

Max did not seem too worried. He was sitting with his knees up to his chin, his arms loosely cradling his legs. In fact, he looked quite relaxed. Was it because he was one of them and therefore had nothing basically to fear? If they were to find and arrest them he would simply produce his identity card. Member of the Secret Police. Or was it because as a student dissident he was used to situations like this and knew that you had to remain cool?

Nik was still see-sawing in his opinion of Max. One moment he thought he could trust him, the next he did not. In the end he had to come back and face the fact that Max hadn't known either of the secret codes. And, as Oscar had kept reminding him, if you can't be sure of someone, don't trust him.

Nik knew that in order to be on the safe side, he would have to get away from Max. But how? The problem had preoccupied him during their travels across the city and was burning a hole in his head right now. The trouble was that they were close together all the time, within touching distance, and Max was strong, stronger than he was. He stood a few centimetres above him, had broader shoulders, a longer reach. Whereas he, Nik, was still growing. He knew that Max would easily be able to wrestle him to the ground.

The police were taking a long time inside the warehouse. The ground was iron cold. Frost sparkled on the roof of the rusted car. Nik moved his shoulders inside his anorak, trying to generate a little heat. Max slipped his hand into his pocket as if to reach for a cigarette, then appeared to think better of it. He must have known that a flaring match might be seen, even the glowing tip of a cigarette.

Suddenly there was a flurry of activity around the warehouse door. The police in the street converged to flank it, like a guard of honour. Nik was aware, though, that there would not be much honour in anything that was about to happen. He raised his head and peered over the top of the car.

Four policemen were emerging from the building, dragging two men who looked like rag dolls, with their heads flopping forward and their feet scarcely brushing the ground. One stumbled, and a policeman struck him on the side of the head with his baton. Nik winced, as if it had been he himself who had been struck, and bit down hard on his lip, tasting blood.

Why did people have to do such terrible things to one another? Surely all this would stop one day? Biba had said that when she was a child they had lived in peace. They had trusted and helped one another. This had been a good country to live in. When travellers came to your door you took them in, gave them a bed for the night and invited them to eat at your table. There had been more to eat then, but not a great deal. It hadn't mattered how much or how little you had, you shared it. Biba remembered how once a man had come all the way from Ireland. He was making a tour of their country on a bicycle. He'd had a small tent strapped to his back carrier, and a billy can to cook his food in. He'd been sleeping in the hills and in barns. He'd said everyone had been kind and hospitable to him. Biba's family had brought him into their cottage and he'd stayed for two whole weeks and helped bring in the hay. 'Ah yes, things were different then,' Biba would say with a sigh. When people lived under a brutal regime, it brutalised them.

The police were bundling the two men into the backs of the cars. The one who had been beaten looked unconscious. His arms hung loose from his shoulders and his legs were all over the place. The police folded him up like a shut knife. Nik glanced at Max. There was no expression on his face at all. None. What a strange, empty, frightening face it looked in the cold moonlight!

Nik made up his mind.

The police clambered back into the cars with a great deal of shouting and slamming of doors. How they love to make a noise! thought Nik. Not like Max who was here beside him. Max moved silently, stealthily, like a fox in the night. Max might be more dangerous than the men in uniforms. They declared themselves. You knew who they were. You knew where you were with them.

The sirens were turned back on, the gleaming red roof lights began to gyrate and the cars sped away, nose to tail, to be swallowed up by the night.

'Sounds like they've gone.' Max yawned and stretched. 'I'll do a little recce and then we can get on our way. You wait here, Nik, until I give you the nod.'

They got to their feet. Nik waited by the car as

instructed, while Max sprinted across the yard towards the boarded-up sales shack on the edge of the forecourt. From there he would be able to get a clear view of the street.

When Max reached the shack, Nik moved. He had done his own recce, had seen a gaping hole in the yard wall behind him. He pushed off the balls of his feet and went like a rocket towards it.

'Come back, you little bastard!' Max yelled.

Nik had his foot in the gap, was gripping with both hands the crumbling stone on either side. He launched himself through with such force that when he landed on the other side he all but stumbled and went flying headlong. He had jarred his right knee, but he managed to keep his feet and regain his balance. He began to run.

He was in a back alley behind a row of houses. He caught a glimpse of their jumbled roofs against the indigo-dark sky. The moon went behind a cloud. He was grateful for that. He heard Max coming behind him, but did not look round.

He emerged from the alley into a deserted street. Terraced houses lined it on either side. All were dark. The only two people alive in the world might have been him and his pursuer. Nik sprinted along the pavement, keeping close to the walls of the houses. They had no gardens. His heels sounded like drumbeats on the pavement.

At the end of the street, he came to a T-junction. He could go right, left, or straight on. He turned left, found himself in a short street.

As soon as he had gone a few metres he realized he was in a cul-de-sac! His eyes widened in horror at the high blank wall that was looming up in front of him.

'Boy!'

He braked abruptly. He turned his head. The voice had been soft, not much more than a whisper. The door of the end house was standing invitingly open.

WEDNESDAY: *MORNING*

Lara dreamt once more her dream of burning, and rose early in the morning with one thought in her mind.

'I'm going to go and find my parents' grave,' she told Nina. In her dream she had seen them, behind a wall of leaping flame. They had been holding out their hands to her.

'It might help set your mind at peace about them. The day is going to be fine. Look, the sun is coming up! Take some flowers from the garden. There are some pretty white narcissi by the hedge. And you'll need something to put them in.'

Lara picked the flowers, damp with dew, their petals not yet unfurled for the day, and gently wrapped them in a sheet of newspaper. Nina gave her an old tin from her carefully hoarded store of tins and bottles and pieces of paper.

'I expect Nik will be here by the time you come back,' said Nina.

Lara hugged her. 'You always look on the bright side, Nina!'

'Why not? It helps. It's easier to live with hope than without.'

The cemetery where Lara's parents were buried was on the edge of the city, about two kilometres from Birch Street. Nina drew a map to show her how to find it. Lara walked there easily. Small groups of men had reappeared to sit around glowing braziers. They sat warming their hands and talking. They looked like workers. They must be on strike! Things were happening. You could smell it in the air, even out here in the suburbs.

The graveyard had once been a country one, before the city had encroached on it, and still had that aspect. It was small in area. Tall, dark green fir trees, close-planted, fringed the edges, sheltering it from fierce winds, keeping it private. Spring flowers bloomed on the graves. There were no big, upstanding, gloomy headstones. The graves were marked with simply made crosses bearing the names of the deceased.

The cemetery was deserted. Lara walked up and down the rows of graves until she found the names of her parents and grandparents. There they were, on one cross: Simon and Sophia, her father's parents. And on the same grave, on another cross: Mark and Lara. She had been called after her mother.

She had noticed a rusted water tap by the back wall. Water gushed from it surprisingly clean and sparkling looking. Lara filled Nina's tin right to the brim, then carried it steadily back to the grave, holding it well out from her body, taking care to lose no more than the odd drop. She wanted the narcissi to have a good long drink and stay fresh as long as possible. They smelt sharp. And, yes, spring-like! She was glad it was spring and that the long bitter winter was behind them.

When she had arranged the flowers in the tin, she placed them at the foot of the grave. Then she spread the newspaper on the damp grass and knelt to tidy the plot. She was surprised how few weeds there were. None of the graves looked neglected. Somebody must care for them. It was unlikely that the authorities would pay anyone to look after them.

A patch of pale yellow primroses was blooming on her parents' grave. She brushed the petals gently with her fingertips, and their soft, light green leaves. They felt so fragile. Yet how sturdy they were! Here they grew in the cold earth, swaying a little in the breeze, bending towards the earth, but unbroken. They made her think of the people of her country. Many of them were bent over, even badly damaged, but their spirit survived and they were ready always to lift up their faces to the sun.

It was only after Lara had finished her tidying and had sat back on her heels that the tears came. She allowed them to flow down her cheeks, unchecked. The grave disappeared in a blur and she saw the faces of her mother and father smiling at her. She reached out a hand to try to touch them.

'Weep, child!' said a voice behind her. 'Let your tears come. And then let the past go.' She felt a hand on her head.

She twisted round to look up into the face of an old man with a white beard. For a moment she thought it was God himself come down from heaven! But he was only an old, shabbily dressed man. Biba had once said, wryly, that theirs was a country of the old and the young; the ones in the middle had been taken away or eliminated.

Lara got up, pulling out a handkerchief to dry her eyes.

'I didn't want to disturb you,' he said. 'But I did want to comfort you.'

She nodded. He had a comforting sort of face. 'Is it you who looks after the graves?'

'It is. I spend a lot of time here.'

'So *you* don't forget the past?'

'I'm old. I have too many memories. But you're young. You're Lara, aren't you? I knew your mother. And your father. You don't remember me?'

As Lara stared at him, a glimmer of recognition began to come.

'I was the priest who helped bury your father.'

'Of course! I remember you now!'

There was nothing about his clothing to suggest he was a priest. He wore a black coat over scuffed corduroy trousers, with a blue, knitted woollen scarf wound around his neck, tucked under his beard. On his head he had a blue woollen hat to match. He would not dare go out in public in clerical garb. The church had been outlawed by the state for many years, though services still went on in private, behind locked doors.

Lara put her hand into her anorak pocket and brought out the little packet that she always carried with her. From it she took her two photographs. She passed them to the priest.

He nodded. 'These are excellent likenesses. They were lovely people, your parents, Lara. Good people. You can feel proud to be their daughter.'

A curtain of spring rain swept suddenly across the graveyard.

'Come into the church, Lara! It's open. We can shelter there.'

They hastened into the little wooden church that kept guard at the edge of the cemetery. The hinges of the door creaked when they opened it and the lock was broken, but the wood floor had been swept clean and there were flowers on the little bench in the nave where previously the altar would have been. The pews had been removed. Jagged holes in the floor showed where they had been ripped out.

They sat down on the floor and rested their backs against the wall. Rain pattered on the arched roof. Lara found herself telling the priest about her life since her mother had died, and about Nik, and why they were here in the city. She told him about Oscar, too. She knew she could trust him. There were some people whom you knew instinctively you could trust.

'Nina thinks we're going to get our freedom. But she's an optimist. What do you think?'

'Ah, freedom!' He sighed. 'It's a big word.'

'Don't you want us to be free?'

'No one is ever quite free, Lara. Something else will enchain us.'

'Such as?'

'The need to make money. To have what other people have.'

'You're talking as though you'd prefer us to stay as we are!'

'No, no! Of course I think we must be rid of this regime. It's brutal and corrupt. Though the corruption may not be so easy to root out. Greedy people

85

are good at surviving, like weeds.' He patted her hand. 'Don't look sad, child. I'm sure your future will be brighter than your parents' was. It's just that people talk as if everything will be solved once we gain our freedom. But it won't be.'

'You'd be able to open your church again, wouldn't you?'

'Yes, I would. I hope to live long enough to see my little church reconsecrated and restored.'

The rain had stopped as abruptly as it started. They rose and went out to see the graveyard looking refreshed from the downpour. The sun had come out. Raindrops glistened like little strings of glass beads along the branches of the trees. A slight mist rose from the grass. And, as they watched, a perfect rainbow, with all seven colours clearly visible, arched over the spire of the church.

They turned to one another and smiled.

'Little things can make us happy, Lara.'

She nodded.

'Come back and see me again, child.'

'I will!' she promised.

She walked home with a more buoyant step, and on the way did a little scavenging for firewood. She picked up some twigs for kindling, found an old chair leg and part of a broken vegetable box, and was well pleased with herself.

When she turned into Birch Street, she stopped dead on the corner. The police patrol car was back, sitting outside Nina's house.

When the door of the house closed behind him, Nik suffered a moment's panic. He might well have jumped from the frying pan into the fire. Here he was in an unknown house, standing in a pitch-dark hall, and he couldn't even see the person who was speaking to him!

'Follow me, lad!' The man clicked on a torch that he held at waist level.

Committed now, and unable to retreat, Nik did as he was told. He followed the bobbing torch and the man's legs into a room full of dancing shadows. In the ghostly light he saw the man's hands swiftly peel back the edge of a carpet, then lift up what looked like a section of the floor.

'Go down there! Stay till I come back for you. And don't worry – it'll be all right.' He broke off as they heard a bang on the front door and an impatient voice raised.

'Open up!'

'Max,' whispered Nik.

'Be quick!' said the man. 'You'll have to jump!'

Nik jumped. Talk about a leap in the dark! Landing he felt soft earth under his feet. The hatch was replaced, and he was plunged into total darkness. He must be in a cellar. Feeling a thin draught of air he groped his way towards it. He ran his hand over the rough wall until he found the vent through which the air was coming. At least he would not suffocate.

What would Oscar have to say about his seeking sanctuary in the house – the cellar – of an unknown, unseen, nameless man? He'd had little choice. He might not have had his back up against the wall exactly, but he had been facing one. A high, blank one that had offered no footholds. And there had been no time to ask for passwords. Do you know Peter Frank? Imagine, with someone snapping at your heels!

Nik squatted on the floor. Something was happening overhead. It felt as if a herd of trampling elephants was passing over. Perhaps his host had lured him in only to hand him over to Max after all! Perhaps he was rolling back the carpet even now and in a moment the hatch would be lifted and he would see them peering down at him, cowering in a corner like a trapped animal.

But the trampling moved away and stillness returned to his underground refuge. He imagined the man taking Max on a tour of the house, going from room to room, opening cupboards, flashing his torch into their dark recesses.

After another few minutes had passed, he felt movement above him again. Then a shaft of light penetrated the darkness.

The man said, 'You can come up now. He's gone.'

Nik took the hand he held out and was pulled up into the light. A paraffin lamp had been lit. In its soft yellow glow Nik saw that the man was middle-aged, with round pebbly glasses and thinning hair.

'You can't stay here, I'm afraid. He might come back. They're wily, they wait, then pounce again. But I'll help you on your way. First, though, can I ask you some questions?'

Nik nodded.

'Do you know Peter Frank?'

Nik smiled. 'I have never heard of him,' he replied.

'He has a sister Hilda.'

'Now that name rings a bell! I think I may have met her at a party, with her sister Lena.'

'Good, good!' said the man.

Nik now said, 'The wind seems to be rising.'

'It always does at night.'

'It will fan the fires.'

'Night fires burn brightest.'

They shook hands.

'Don't tell me your name, boy. I don't need to know.'

'But why did you call me in from the street? You didn't know who I was.'

'I could see you were just a boy. And that a man was after you. I heard your footsteps – yours and his. I'd been watching for someone else, a messenger. When you see someone being pursued, you know he's in deadly trouble.'

'Are you part of the network?'

'I am. It's wide, you know. Wider than the authorities think. That's part of our strength. I'm going to send you on to other people who can help you.'

He took Nik to the back door. 'Go down the lane here to the left. Knock on the fifth door on the right-hand side and say that Luke sent you. And good luck!'

'Thank you. Thank you very much!'

The man closed the door.

Nik waited until his eyes had adjusted to yet another change of light, then he moved stealthily down the lane. He was moving as Max moved, he realized, walking on the balls of his feet, keeping his back half-turned to the wall, so that he could flatten himself against it if necessary. He could also watch to the right or the left of him. His right eye was twitching. Nerves. He took a deep breath. He was aware that Max could be lurking in the shadows.

He counted the doors on the right-hand side and when he reached the fifth one he knocked gently. Too gently, he decided, when nothing happened. He knocked again. This time he feared he had knocked too loudly. The noise might have been heard right along the lane.

Almost immediately a voice spoke to him through a grille in the door.

'Who is there?'

'Luke sent me.'

The door was opened on a short chain. Nik was asked for the passwords. They went through the two sequences, and he was admitted by a young man, who looked about Oscar's age.

'Go ahead,' he said to Nik.

Nik went down a short passage and found himself in a small kitchen, lit by one hanging bulb shaded with blue paper. A girl was sitting curled up in an armchair, drinking something from a cup. She looked cold in the blue light. Her hands were cradled round the cup as if to warm them.

The man said, 'My name is Jan. And this is Sophie.'

'I'm Nik.'

'Sit down, Nik,' said Sophie, 'and I'll make you some tea. Dandelion all right?'

'Yes, please.'

Jan perched on a stool in front of Nik. 'So, you know Luke?'

'Not really.' Nik told them how Luke had helped him. 'This man Max is probably still in the area looking for me,' he added anxiously.

Jan asked him to describe Max and when Nik did, he nodded. 'I think we've run across this person ourselves. He uses different names on different occasions. He's reputed to be one of the most highly esteemed and feared of the Secret Police agents. He dresses like a student, poses as one.'

'How did you come across him?' Sophie put a mug of hot tea into Nik's hand.

'I was taking a message to Stefan Bild.'

'Poor Stefan!' Jan shook his head. 'And how did you come to know *him*?'

'I'm a friend of Oscar's.'

'Oscar Lind?'

'Yes.'

'We've been worried sick about Oscar,' said Sophie. 'We saw he'd been hit, but we haven't been able to find out any news of him. How is he?'

'Recovering.'

'Good!'

'Could you take us to him, Nik, in the morning?' asked Jan. 'We have plans we need to discuss.'

It seemed that everyone wanted to be taken to Oscar.

WEDNESDAY: *11.00 a.m.*

The police car outside Nina's house belonged to their 'friendly' policeman. But was he really friendly or not? Perhaps, when he'd called before, he had been trying to get in with them, to gain their confidence, and had come now about his real business. Oscar.

There was no sign of Oscar when Lara came into the kitchen. The policeman was sitting by the table with his cap off and his tunic unbuttoned, drinking a cup of tea.

'Ah, there you are, Lara!' His greeting was warm. 'I was just asking where you were.'

'I told him you'd gone to visit your parents' grave.' Nina looked searchingly at Lara's face. 'Are you all right, dear?'

'Fine.' And Lara realized that she was, except for her anxiety about the policeman.

'A cup of tea?'

'Please.'

'Our friend here came to bring us a piece of bacon.' Nina nodded at a parcel lying on the draining board. 'That was kind of him, wasn't it?'

'Very kind.' Lara relaxed a little.

'I promised I'd bring you a bit if any came my way.' He shifted over at the table. 'Come on and sit here by me, Lara. I was telling my Marta about you.'

Lara took the chair next to him.

'It's a terrible thing for you to have lost two parents by your age. Was it an accident that took the two of them?'

'No,' she said, and paused. He was waiting for her to go on. 'My mother was ill. She was never strong.'

'You poor child! And what about your father?'

What *about* her father? She couldn't tell him he had been shot by the Secret Police.

Nina butted in. 'He was also taken by an illness. But Lara was too young at the time to know much about it.'

'So after they died you came to live here with your Aunt Nina?'

Lara glanced at Nina. What should she say? If she said 'yes', he might discover afterwards that she'd been an inmate at the orphanage and had been lying. Once you started to lie, it seemed you had to go on. It was out of the question, though, to tell the truth.

Again, Nina answered for her. 'Yes, she came to live with me.'

'It was good that she had you!'

He stayed long enough only to drink his tea, then he buttoned up his jacket and said he must be off. He had work to do. They were being kept on the hop these days! Neither Nina nor Lara made any comment.

'That was a good cup of tea! I feel the better for it.'

Nina and Lara went with him to the door.

'Thank you again for the bacon,' said Nina. 'We'll enjoy it, won't we, Lara?'

'Oh yes, yes we will! Very much.'

'If I get a few eggs I'll let you have some of those, too.'

'Oh, we wouldn't like to trouble you further,' said Nina. 'And you have your own family to consider.'

'They get plenty.'

On the outside step, he paused. 'I was up at the orphanage yesterday, Nina,' he said, looking her in the eye. 'I met your sister.'

'Biba?'

How can Nina stay so calm? wondered Lara. She herself was trembling.

He nodded. 'The director and matron have made off. And so it seems have some of the pupils.' He set his cap on his head. 'Well, I'll be seeing you. Take care of yourselves now!'

When they had closed the door, Lara said, 'He knows!'

'Yes, I think he does.' Nina spoke quietly. 'And he was letting us know that he does.'

'But why did he go to the orphanage?'

'The police must know Oscar is Biba's grandson. But she won't have given any information away, if she had any to give.'

'So what are we going to do?' cried Lara.

'Nothing. What can we do?'

'But what is this man up to? Is he our friend or not, Nina?'

'It's difficult to say, dear.'

'Should I go up and tell Oscar he can come down?'

'Better wait.'

They returned to the kitchen. Lara lifted the cups from the table and took them over to the sink to rinse. As she turned on the tap she raised her head to look out of the window and thought she saw somebody move behind the low wall that separated the back garden from the canal walkway.

'Nina, I think there's someone out there!'

Nina joined her at the window. There was nothing to be seen now except for a blackbird sitting on the wall with his beak up in the air, gobbling. A fat pink worm was vanishing fast into the yellow beak.

'It could be another policeman,' said Lara. 'Watching the house.'

'It could be. Just carry on with what you're doing. Try not to look bothered.'

Nina lifted the piece of bacon and unwrapped it. She sniffed it, put it into a pot and ran in water. Then she dropped in a pinch of dried thyme that had come from her own garden. 'There's nothing like a few herbs to add flavour, Lara. It's a good joint, is it not?' She fussed over it, as if nothing else in the world was concerning her.

Lara finished washing the cups. When she was taking the drying-up cloth from its hook she stole another quick look into the garden. She saw something move again behind the wall. And this time she was in no doubt.

'There *is* someone out there, Nina!'

'Well, all right. Come away from the window, then, dear. And run upstairs and warn Oscar to stay where he is.'

Lara threw down the cloth and went racing up the stairs, taking two and three at a time.

'Oscar!' she called, when she reached the top landing.

The hatch above her opened a fraction.

'Stay where you are! We think the police may be watching the house.'

'Okay!' The hatch snapped back into place.

Lara sped back down the stairs. She heard voices in the kitchen!

She took a deep breath before she opened the door.

Nina was standing in the centre of the floor laughing. She turned to Lara.

'It's Nik! That's who it was who was skulking behind the wall! Nik, with a couple of friends!'

WEDNESDAY: *MIDDAY*

Oscar came down to join them. He hugged Nik, Sophie and Jan in turn.

'It's good to see all three of you!'

Nik could relax now. He had felt ninety-nine per cent sure about Jan and Sophie, but that remaining one per cent had kept his anxiety on the boil while they were making their way across the city.

Nina was filling the kettle.

'It's time now to lay plans,' said Oscar. 'I've already spent too many hours cooped up in the attic!'

So the talking began.

Nik and Lara took turns to keep watch from the upstairs window, while Nina kept guard at the back. They had to be on extra special alert. If the patrol car were to return, they would have to act very fast. Four people would now have to make their get-away up the stairs into the attic.

'We've got to bring all the people back together in the square, as before,' said Oscar.

They were ready, Jan told him. 'They're not going to give up this time. They're as restless as we are.'

More and more workers were going on strike, reported Sophie, who had been out gathering news and gossip from different sources. She'd been to offices, factories, hospitals, community centres. On the whole it was easier for girls to move freely around the city. Most male students were regarded as suspect.

'Though there were plenty of girls and women in the square that night!' said Sophie.

Lara nodded. She had been there herself, after all, hadn't she?

Sophie had also heard that unrest in the army and police was still mounting.

'The trouble is knowing which ones are for us and which are against,' said Nina.

'Exactly!' said Oscar.

He sat at the head of the table, his face flushed, his eyes glowing, suggesting he might be a little fevered. Lara could see that Nina was longing to fuss over him, to tell him to watch his strength, but was restraining herself. Fully recovered or not, Oscar was determined to be at the centre of any action.

'Now for some practical matters,' he said.

The first priority was to get leaflets printed and distributed. Oscar stressed it was essential to cover every part of the city.

They wrote the copy for the leaflet on the kitchen table.

'On Saturday evening at six o'clock,' it said, 'there will be a massive demonstration in Cathedral Square.' It called upon all citizens to come out and support it.

By this time, Nina's bacon joint was ready. It had been bubbling away on the stove and the tantalising smell had been filling the kitchen, making their mouths water. They tidied away the papers and Nina set in front of them a steaming dish of bacon, potatoes and onions.

'A feast, Nina!' Oscar shook his head in wonder. 'I haven't seen such good food in a long time!'

'You can thank your policeman,' said Nina.

Oscar burnt the paper on which he'd written the copy for the leaflet. As he said, they were unlikely to forget the message.

After they'd eaten, Sophie and Lara set out carrying two large oilskin shopping bags apiece. The bags were empty, except for some rags Nina had given them from her store. The girls might have been going to market.

They walked briskly in the direction of the Markets area, then turned off just before reaching it into a narrow back street. At an unmarked door, Sophie stopped and knocked. She spoke to someone through the letter-box, and the door opened.

They went into a room that looked as if it had once been a laundry. Big, deep-sided stone tubs were ranged along one wall and overhead dangled two bars of a broken pulley. A number of students were in the room, gathered around an old printing press. There was a pungent smell of ink.

Sophie introduced Lara and explained why they had come.

'We'll do it straight away. No problem!'

'Have you enough paper?'

'We got a big stack from the university office this morning, and more ink.'

Sophie and Lara sat on upturned boxes to wait while one of the students set up the type. After that the printing could begin. When the leaflets began to roll off the press they looked a bit smudgy, but were legible enough. The girls spread them out to dry, then they gathered and stacked them. The bundles covered the floor in tottering, daunting piles.

Two of the students offered to help by doing a couple of runs. The rest could not be spared. They were in the middle of preparing a student newsletter.

'We've got to keep spreading information,' said the student in charge of the press. 'Watch how you go now, you two! It's dangerous, you realize, don't you, what you're doing? If you're stopped and searched, you'll be arrested on the spot.'

'We'd better not be stopped then, had we?' said Sophie.

They crammed their shopping bags full of leaflets and arranged Nina's rags on top.

They decided to start with the area in the immediate vicinity, planning to move outward in ever widening circles. They took out one leaflet at a time, folded it and put it through each letter box they passed, or else, with a quick dip at the knees they bent down and slipped it under the door. They tried to perform the operation casually and without being seen. It was easier in a row of terraced houses sitting straight on to the pavement, more difficult when they had to go up a path to the front door.

Some people must have noticed what they were doing, but no one looked at them openly. They saw faces watching from behind curtains and Lara sensed, once or twice, someone standing on the other side of the door while she was pushing the leaflet through. Easing back the letter flap she saw the person's foot. As she let the flap drop back into place she imagined the man or woman stooping to lift up the leaflet.

They worked one side of a street, then moved together into the next. They did several streets, returned to the press with their empty bags, picked up more leaflets and set out again without stopping to rest. Soon their legs and shoulders were aching, yet they seemed only to have dented the pile of leaflets.

During one run they came upon a block of smart apartments, with wrought-iron balconies and fresh paint gleaming on the window frames. An air of quiet pervaded the well-kept surrounding lawns and flower borders. As Lara made to go up the path, Sophie caught hold of her arm.

'No, Lara, don't go there!'

'No?'

'No. They'll be government apartments, for "in" people. Government employees, security forces, spies, and the like. When you see anything as attractive-looking as this you know it'll be occupied by supporters of the regime.'

While Sophie was speaking, a man had come out of the building. He was carrying a walkie-talkie. He accosted them.

'What are you two doing hanging about here?'

'We were just admiring the gardens,' said Sophie.

'You've admired them now, so get moving!' The man's gaze travelled from their faces down to their bags. He had suspicious eyes.

They moved. They were conscious of his eyes boring into them as they walked off along the pavement.

'Don't look back!' said Sophie. '*Don't!*'

When they had turned the corner, they ran.

At the end of the next street, they found a group of striking workers sitting by a huge, fiercely-burning fire on a vacant lot. They passed the leaflets round the circle.

'We'll be there on Saturday,' the men promised. 'You can count on us!'

'It's a wonder the police haven't moved you on,' remarked Sophie.

'It is, isn't it? Plenty have been past. But they seem to be turning a blind eye.'

'Why are they, do you think?'

'It's too big a job for them, trying to put down a whole nation. For that's what it's come to. Especially when not all their hearts are in it.'

Lara hoped that the man was right. A few minutes later, they came face to face with two policemen on foot patrol. One of the men was holding a German wolfhound on a short leash.

The dog immediately began to sniff at the girls' bags. It had wicked looking teeth and a nasty glint in its eye.

'Where are you two girls going?'

'We've been looking for food. No luck, I'm afraid.' Sophie shrugged.

'We've had a report that two girls are in the area distributing leaflets. Subversive leaflets. You wouldn't happen to know anything about that, by any chance?' The policeman also had a nasty glint in his eye.

'We haven't noticed any girls, have we, Lara?'

The dog was now trying to push its head into Lara's bag.

'Let's have a look in those bags!'

The dog was ordered off. It sat back on its haunches with its tongue lolling.

The girls held the bags open and the policemen scrabbled amongst the rags until their fingers reached the bottom.

'Okay then, on your way!'

When the policemen had gone, Lara said, 'Thank goodness we'd given the last of the leaflets to the men at the bonfire!'

THURSDAY

Lara and Nik wanted to go out on their own next day to deliver leaflets.

'I'm not sure about that,' said Oscar. Nor, from the look on her face, was Nina.

'We'll be very careful,' promised Nik.

'We'll be all right, really we will,' said Lara. 'And we'll probably attract less attention than Sophie and Jan, with us being younger.'

'High school students are regarded as suspect, too,' said Nina sharply.

'We can't just sit in the house doing *nothing*,' objected Lara.

'Lara does know the drill,' put in Sophie. 'And she's sharp.'

'Oh, all right!' Oscar gave in.

He himself was to stay in the house, directing operations. He still had his spells of weakness, though would not admit to them. But at least he would remain under Nina's watchful eye.

Nik and Lara set off for the printing press with

Jan and Sophie. The two younger ones were given a large suburban area to cover quite far out from the city centre. Less dangerous than the centre, said Jan. He advised them to take the bus, and gave them a handful of coins.

The buses were running infrequently and they had to queue sometimes for as much as half an hour. People peered at their bags, which they'd filled to the point that they could barely lift them. They had to hump them up and down the bus step.

'Dirty laundry,' Lara told those who were curious. 'Not food.' That was what would be in their minds. Beyond this exchange, Lara held her tongue and discouraged conversation, which normally she would have fallen into happily. Nik's way of dealing with people's nosiness was to stare straight ahead.

The buses, when they did come, were jam-packed and their windows steamed up. The air smelt sour. People were irritable and cursed their bulging bags, which took up space. They had to stand with their legs braced and the bags held protectively between them.

It rained on and off throughout the day. The weather had been tempestuous and changeable for the last two or three days; one moment it was spring, and the next, showers of freezing rain and hail lashed the streets, sending them scurrying for shelter under archways and into doorways.

They leafleted first an estate of high flats where the lifts were broken and half the windows boarded over. The corridors and stairways stank and were littered with rubbish. Mould grew on inside walls. Outside, sickly trees and shrubs struggled to survive;

many had been wrenched from their roots. Two youths on a rooftop pelted them with stones as they walked between the blocks. They had to run. The youths were not likely to be supporters of the President, just vandals and troublemakers.

They were glad after that to come into a district of older, one and two-storeyed houses. Flowers bloomed in these gardens, unmolested; the trees were beginning to come into bud.

As they were approaching the door of one house, it was opened by a man who engaged them in conversation and invited them in for a cup of tea.

'You look in need of one!'

They hesitated. He'd told them his name and that he was a teacher. He taught chemistry at the local high school. He was at home, since the schools were closed.

They were damp, leg-weary and thirsty, and Lara needed to go to the lavatory.

She turned to Nik. 'What do you think?' she mouthed. The man, who was called Carl, looked trustworthy.

Nik nodded. They'd decided on their travels around the city that most of its citizens were for them. Few wanted the President and his men.

They went in.

Carl directed Lara to the bathroom and when she opened the door she got a pleasant surprise. The place both looked and smelled clean and it had a lavatory that flushed! Nina's did not, neither did any in the orphanage. They had to be flushed with cans of water; the cisterns had broken down years ago. And there was a roll of soft pink paper beside the toilet, instead of the usual newspaper squares stuck on a spike.

Lara washed her hands with the sweet-smelling bar of pale pink soap shaped like a sea-shell and dried her hands on the pale pink fluffy towel hanging on the rail. How had Carl got these things? Did he work for the government? A stab of fear shot through her. Perhaps they'd been foolish to come in. When you were tired, it was easier to make mistakes.

Once they began to talk, her anxieties were allayed. Carl had relatives in the West, in America and England, who regularly sent parcels. That was how he and his wife had acquired a few luxuries. That was how most people got a few extras.

Carl's wife was at work. She was a physicist at a government research station.

'Though she's not for the government, not by any means!' Carl told them that everyone they knew – friends, neighbours, colleagues, senior pupils at his school – would be in the square on Saturday. 'Almost everyone,' he corrected himself. 'Our next-door neighbour will not. Don't put a leaflet through her door! She works at the Intercontinental Hotel as a spy. She spies on the foreign guests. She sits in the corridor and when they go out she nips into their rooms and rakes through their stuff.'

'How do you know?' asked Lara.

'It's common knowledge. The guests' rooms are bugged and the Secret Service men sit on the third floor listening in to their conversations. The third floor is given over to them.'

When they were getting ready to leave, Carl offered the loan of two bicycles. 'They're no great shakes. Or perhaps I should say that they are! They're real bone-rattlers. But they'll get you there faster than your feet.'

They accepted his offer gratefully.

He came with them to the gate. Lara glanced apprehensively at his neighbour's house, but Carl said they needn't worry about her at the moment. She would be at the hotel. She worked from eight in the morning until eight in the evening, then came home in a taxi and staggered up the path laden down with bags full of food from the hotel kitchens.

'Good luck, then!' he said.

They thanked him and Lara promised they'd bring back the bikes afterwards.

'There's no hurry.'

'Afterwards!' said Lara to Nik as they rode away, wobbling somewhat. One of her tyres was flat and Nik's handlebars were stuck at twenty to two. The bike kept wanting to peel off to the left. The brakes on neither machine were particularly good. 'I can't imagine how it's going to be, can you, *after*wards?'

'Not really.'

'Of course we don't even know if the uprising will be successful, do we?'

'It's got to be successful!' said Nik fiercely.

After delivering their last load of leaflets for the day on the fringe of the city, they realized they were only a couple of kilometres or so from the orphanage. On the bikes they could be there in a few minutes.

'Shall we go?' Lara was already poised in the saddle.

Nik nodded.

Out on the country road their legs seemed to find a new burst of energy. They whizzed along, bouncing over the pot-holes, laughing when water swooshed up over their legs. For a short while they forgot about the impending uprising. Only two cars passed them, both private.

'Won't we give Biba a surprise!' said Lara. She had released her hair and the wind was whipping it straight out behind her. What a sense of liberation it gave her just to feel her hair flowing free!

The gates of the orphanage stood open. The grounds were deserted. There was nothing unusual in that. Many of the children hated to go outside on their own and Biba wouldn't have time to take them. Lara and Nik used to play games with the little ones in the garden. They played chasey and leap frog and singing games in a ring, but not hide-and-seek. The children were too fearful to hide.

Lara cycled ahead of Nik up the drive. She couldn't wait to go rushing in and shout, 'Surprise, surprise!' and fling her arms around Biba.

She threw the bike down on to the grass verge and ran up to the big, heavy front door. She gave it a push, but it wouldn't budge.

'It's locked.'

'Biba wouldn't want strangers wandering in.'

'They wouldn't have taken them all away, would they?' Lara felt suddenly alarmed.

'I can't see why they would. Where would they take them?' But Nik began to feel just a little worried, too. The place did seem terribly quiet.

He lifted the letter-box flap and they inclined their ears.

'I can hear a baby crying!' said Lara with relief. 'It must be all right, mustn't it?'

Nik was still looking undecided. 'I suppose.'

'Well, why not?'

'I guess I'm just getting cautious, like everybody else. It's infectious. Let's go round the back.'

They left the bikes and went round the side, instinctively keeping close to the bushes. The back door was ajar.

'Wait!' Nik held back Lara, who had been on the brink of running forward. He had spied something behind a fat holly bush near the door. Something glinting in the sunshine. Something chrome.

They moved a little closer. Now they could see it was a motor bike that was propped against the wall, half concealed by the bush. No one who had worked at the orphanage had ever owned such a bike. It was big and shinily black and powerful-looking. Such a bike could only be owned by someone who was himself big and powerful.

There were voices coming from the kitchen.

They crept forward until they were only two or three metres from the door. Nik motioned to Lara to crouch down with him behind another bush.

One of the voices was Biba's.

'I'm sorry,' she was saying, 'but I can't help you. I have no idea where he is.'

The next person to speak was a man. 'When did you last see him?'

Nik frowned. The voice sounded familiar. He bent his head and concentrated on listening.

'A few weeks ago.'

'Are you sure?'

'Oh, yes. He came to see me on my birthday. That was back in January.'

'And what about this boy Nik?'

Nik felt as if he had received an electric shock. At his side, Lara jumped, and he had to put a hand over her mouth as he saw it fly open.

'Is *he* a friend of your grandson's?'

Nik knew now to whom the other voice belonged. It was Max who was in the kitchen with Biba.

THURSDAY: *5.30 p.m.*

They took off at speed from the orphanage. Just a kilometre up the road, Lara's flat tyre collapsed completely. She bumped along on the rim for a little way, but it slowed their progress.

'I'm going to wreck the wheel!' She stopped and put both feet down on the road.

'Carl will understand. Hang on!' Nik raised his hand. 'There's something coming. It could be a motor bike.'

They were at the side of their old wood, the one in which they had sought refuge before. Quickly they pushed the bicycles into the undergrowth and squatted down beside them. They were just in time to see a helmeted driver go roaring past on the gleaming black motor bike.

'Max,' said Nik, lifting his head to watch the black speck disappear into the dusk.

'Shall we go back to the orphanage?' said Lara. 'We'd better, hadn't we, to see that Biba's all right?'

'Yes, I think we had. We'll leave Carl's bike here – we can hide it – and I'll take you on my crossbar.'

They turned to look at the western sky. The sun

was dropping behind the low range of blue hills and colour was ebbing fast from the land. They knew it would not be possible to go to the orphanage and get back to the city before curfew.

This time, the back door was locked.

Nik rapped with his knuckles. 'Biba!' he called.

Nothing happened. Behind the door, the big house seemed deadly quiet.

Nik rapped again, more sharply this time, and raised his voice. 'Biba – Biba, it's Nik and Lara!'

Then came the sound of the key grating in the lock. The door opened, and Biba peered out at them, her brow creased with anxiety.

'My goodness!' She put out her plump little hands to them. 'What are the two of you doing here at this time? It's almost six. Come in, come in!' She hugged them, then locked the door behind them. 'I've just had another visitor.'

'We know,' said Lara. 'We saw him.'

'A nasty piece of work he was too! He was asking about Oscar. He searched my room. He pulled it apart and he found the little book where I keep my addresses.' Biba was distressed. 'He saw Nina's name in it. He saw we had the same surname. I didn't tell him a thing. I'd have gone to the stake first.'

Lara put her arm around Biba and comforted her. It was the first time she'd had to comfort Biba. Usually it was the other way round.

Voices were heard approaching, and the soft shuffle of feet. A boy put his head round the door and when he saw Nik and Lara his big dark eyes widened. He dived into the corridor again.

'Nik and Lara are back!' he shouted.

Soon children were flooding into the room, shouting and laughing. Little Katya came to Lara and clasped her around the waist.

'Where have you been?' she demanded. 'Where *were* you?'

'In the town,' laughed Lara.

Within seconds she was surrounded by children plucking at her clothes, clamouring to be picked up, to be cuddled, to be played with, to be read to. They chattered non-stop, like a flock of young sparrows.

'Can we go into the wood in the morning, Lara? *Please*! Can we play games?'

'Read to us in bed, Lara!'

'Can we have the three bears story?'

'I want the one about the big bad wolf!'

Katya said nothing. She just held on tightly to Lara.

'See how they've missed you, Lara!' said Biba.

Nik had gone out to fetch wood for the stove.

'I don't know how I've managed without the two of you!' said Biba. 'You'll stay the night? You'll have to, or else you'll get yourselves arrested.'

Lara and Nik sat on for a while beside the kitchen stove after Biba had gone up to the night nursery. Biba was worried about Paul, one of the younger children. Paul suffered with a bad chest and had never been well since he'd arrived in the orphanage the year before. Biba often sat with him at night helping him to breathe, steaming kettles, crooning to him, rubbing his back. She'd had to manage on her own at nights since Lara and Nik had been away.

111

The kitchen and cleaning staff left in the late afternoon, to be home before curfew.

The small hours of the morning were the most difficult hours at the orphanage, when children who were sick were fretful and needed extra attention. Biba survived on little sleep. She catnapped. She didn't mind that she was never off duty. What would she do with a day off? she would ask. She could always go and visit her sister Nina of course, though she hated the city, never had liked it. Too much traffic. Too many people. Too many soldiers. Nina could come and visit her, she said.

'I hope Nina won't be worrying too much about us,' said Lara. They knew that she would be.

'We'll leave at six sharp in the morning.'

'It feels funny being back.' Lara gazed into the dwindling embers of the fire. 'As if we've been away for much longer than we actually have. Do you think we'll come back afterwards, Nik – to live, I mean?'

'It depends, doesn't it? On what happens. If I find my father –' Nik stopped, shrugged. His face closed up again.

They fell silent, each locked into their own thoughts.

Nik remembered the last glimpse he'd had of his father before he'd been led away. He'd turned to give Nik a nod and even the glimmer of a smile. At this point, always, Nik found he could think no more. He let his mind shift into neutral.

Lara felt suddenly cold. The fire was almost out. She wanted Nik to find his father, of course she did, but if he did, he would probably go up north and live in the country with him. Nik had grandparents alive still, and an uncle and aunt and some cousins. He had a family. The uncle had come once to visit Nik at the orphanage. He'd said he was sorry he couldn't take Nik back with him but he and his wife didn't have enough room as it was. The grandparents lived with them, as well as their children. His wife couldn't cope with anyone else. The uncle had been embarrassed and had not looked Nik in the eye.

'No one wants orphans!' Nik had said afterwards and his face had worn its dark, brooding look. He'd gone for a long walk in the woods and not come back until nightfall. The Crow had given him a beating and Nik had thought of running away. But he'd had nowhere to run to.

'I'd like to go to school,' said Lara now. 'I'd like to get a proper education.'

'I want to be a farmer,' said Nik. 'And work on the land. What about you?'

'I don't know, I'm not sure yet.' Lara shrugged. The future seemed too difficult to contemplate when the present was so pressing.

FRIDAY: *4 a.m.*

In the early hours, Lara was awakened by Nik shaking her and saying, 'Get up, Lara!'

She leapt up, startled. Nik was standing beside her bed, fully clothed. In the long shadowy room, lit by its solitary feeble night-light, the other children slept on in their narrow truckle beds.

For a moment she thought she was still dreaming,

that she was back in that other night – Sunday night – when Nik had wakened her and said, 'The city's burning!' He had wakened her, then, from her own nightmare of burning. She had not dreamed that dream since she'd visited her parents' grave.

'Is the city on fire?' she asked, confused.

'No. It's little Paul. He's in a bad way. Biba wants us to go for the doctor. The telephone's out of order. The Crow disconnected it before he left.'

Lara dressed at once.

Nik and Lara ran down the stairs and took the bicycle from the back scullery where they had left it.

'You go on this one,' said Nik. 'I'll take the old wreck.'

An old bicycle was kept in a shed outside. The brakes didn't work and it had no lights.

It was two kilometres to the village. They bumped over the rutted country road through the dark, moonless night, with only the faint beam from Carl's front lamp to light their way. Bats flew in front of them. They heard the hoot of an owl and the low growl of an unseen dog. No human being appeared to be abroad.

The doctor lived on the edge of the village. His house was dark and silent.

They banged on the door and set a dog barking within. Soon afterwards, the door was opened by the doctor himself, barefooted, and in the middle of pulling on his dressing-gown. He said he would dress and come straight away.

He arrived in his car at the orphanage no more than ten minutes later, but he was too late. Paul had died five minutes before.

FRIDAY: *MORNING*

'I'm sorry.' The doctor raised his hands helplessly. Lara wept in Biba's arms. Nik stood stiffly beside them, his eyes hot and bright.

The death of a child was not an unusual event at the orphanage. Only last month one of the baby girls had died. All the other children – those over eight – had gone to the funeral in the village churchyard. They had carried wreaths of early daffodils plucked from the orphanage grounds. It had been a cheerless, grey day. Rain had fallen unceasingly.

Trudging back through the mud from the cemetery, Biba had been angry. Too many children had died for lack of food and medicine, she said. Their country had been reduced to a total mess.

And now there was another death, and the orphanage would go once more into mourning.

When Lara lay down to try and snatch another hour's sleep before dawn, she came to a decision. She would train to be a doctor. She would help sick children. Children like little Paul. She had thought about it before but had not imagined that someone like her – an orphan – could do it. She still did not know how she would manage it, but she was determined to find a way. Since last Saturday her world had opened up; it was no longer contained by the walls of the orphanage.

Because of the broken night Nik and Lara set off for Birch Street later than they had planned.

'Don't go!' pleaded Katya, who had slept in Lara's bed. 'Please don't go!' She clung to Lara's hand and had to be pried loose by Biba.

'I'll come back, Katya,' promised Lara. 'I came last time, didn't I?'

'To stay for ever and ever? Promise!'

That was a promise Lara was unable to make.

'Just go!' commanded Biba, holding Katya's thin, quivering body firmly against her own rounded one. 'Hush now, love,' she said to the child, breaking off to caution Nik and Lara to go carefully.

They left to the sound of Katya crying.

Nik rode the wreck again. He didn't mind, he said, and his legs were longer than Lara's. He could put his feet to the ground when he needed to stop.

The highway throbbed with the movement of military vehicles. They heard the roar before they reached it. At the edge of the slip road, they paused. A steady line of high-sided, grey-green trucks was making its way into the city. Each truck bristled with helmeted, heavily armed soldiers.

Nik and Lara edged cautiously into the stream of traffic, keeping well in to the side. The convoy was travelling at speed, kicking up a light spray of water from the roadway. Every now and then a truck came too near to be comfortable and the back draught almost blew them off their bikes.

The traffic intensified as they approached the city outskirts. Here, the heavy presence of police cars was helping to add to the feeling of urgency and apprehension. And fear. You could smell the fear in the air, see it in the way that those on foot kept their heads down and scurried along the pavements,

116

anxious not to attract attention. The black and white cars of the city police department were careering through the streets at break-neck speeds with their klaxons screaming and their roof lights flashing as if the uprising had already started. They wove in and out of the traffic, causing even the army trucks to brake, and, as usual, they made no attempt to observe red lights.

'Who do they think they are!' muttered Nik. 'Lunatics! Showing off. Trying to frighten us.'

'One more day,' said Lara. 'And then –!'

She swerved as a police car came alarmingly close. Her front wheel touched Nik's and they collided, falling in a heap together into the gutter. For a brief moment, they sat there, looking at one another, feeling that the effort to rise might be too much. Then swiftly they disentangled themselves and got back on to their feet, before they and the bikes would be mashed to pieces. Carl's machine now had a twisted back wheel.

'Another casualty!' said Nik.

They walked for a bit, pushing the bikes along the outside edge of the pavement, and after that walked and rode alternately, a short distance at a time. There seemed to be few private cars about, and no buses. A woman at a pedestrian crossing told them that the drivers were on strike.

'The factory workers are out as well.'

Shops were boarded up, and their doors padlocked.

Skirting the city centre Nik and Lara passed the modern multi-storeyed Intercontinental Hotel and thought of Carl's neighbour skulking along the

117

passages, snooping in the guests' rooms. Carl was right about the windows of the third floor: they were blanked out.

Once they left the Markets area behind, the traffic began to thin out and they could ride again without fear of being mown down. The caterwauling of klaxons and horns faded gradually into the distance.

Now they were on the home stretch and the corner of Birch Street was in sight. They pedalled faster. Soon they would be safe inside Nina's snug little kitchen, with the kettle hissing and Nina fussing over them.

When they reached the corner, they pulled up so sharply that Lara almost went over the handlebars. The scene in front of them left them gasping.

The street was buzzing with activity, and most of it appeared to be concentrated outside number twenty-seven. At the kerb stood four police cars, parked nose to tail, as if they'd been driven at speed and stopped abruptly. Behind them was a black van with grilled windows, while across the road crouched two long grey vans bearing the logo of the state-controlled television company. Swarms of policemen were prowling up and down the pavements on either side.

And right in the middle of the road, a man on a skid board was training a large film camera on Nina's yellow door.

FRIDAY: *MIDDAY*

Nik and Lara retreated. They moved back to a position where they would have partial cover behind a hedge but still keep a view of the street.

They noticed several other cameramen were waiting on the pavement, with smaller, hand-held cameras.

'Press!' whispered Nik.

All newspapers, like television, were state-controlled.

Something was about to happen at number twenty-seven. The air had become charged as if a bolt of electricity had been released. Lara and Nik sensed it even from where they stood. A gold-braided officer barked an order and the rest of the police converged on Nina's gate to flank it. They stood with legs braced and hand guns cocked. The film camera began to roll, the pressmen moved into position. Lara clutched Nik's arm.

The yellow door opened, and out came two policemen dressed in riot gear, followed by two in plain clothes who were half carrying, half dragging a man. The captive looked limp in their hands. His shirt was torn and there was blood on his face. His head flopped, his red hair was tousled.

Oscar blinked, startled, as flashbulbs exploded one after the other in his face. His arrest was being well recorded, and would be widely reported.

Today the last vestiges of the student revolt were extinguished with the arrest of . . .

One of the plain-clothes policemen was wearing a black reefer jacket.

'Bastard!' said Nik.

Lara put her hand over Nik's mouth and held on to him. In another second he might have gone dashing forward and ended up in the arms of the police himself.

Oscar was being bundled into the back of the high black van. He slipped and half fell as he went up the step. Max put out his hand and gave him a shove, sending him sprawling on the van floor. Lara winced, Nik's mouth tightened. Then Max leapt in behind Oscar, followed by the other plain-clothes policeman. The doors were slammed shut.

The uniformed police piled into their cars and the drivers began to fire up the engines.

'Hadn't we better get out of here?' said Lara.

But where could they go?

The first police car was already pulling out from the kerb.

'Over the hedge!' cried Nik.

They rolled over the prickly top and landed on the soft earth of someone's garden. Through gaps in the screen, they watched the procession sweep past.

When the sound of sirens had died away, they clambered back over the hedge, doing their best not to mangle it. They abandoned the bikes and made for the canal which ran behind the street, on Nina's side.

It was quiet on the towpath. Even the birds seemed to have fallen silent. The brackish water lay sluggish and undisturbed, except for a couple of empty oil drums that were rolling gently in mid-stream. Sodden cigarette packets and bashed tins lay trapped in the scummy foam along the edges. The canal was polluted from chemical waste disgorged by factories along its banks. 'Fall into the canal,' Nina had told them, 'and the poison will invade your whole body'.

They made their way carefully along the path, their feet squelching in the grey mud. They walked hunched over, keeping their heads below the level of the wall that separated the canal from the back gardens of the street. When they reached Nina's house, they straightened up.

There, framed in the kitchen window, were Nina's head and shoulders. Her shoulders were moving in bustly fashion; she must be washing something in the sink. Trust Nina to be up and doing and not sitting around lamenting! Her forehead, though, was ridged below her kerchief.

Nik whistled softly.

Nina looked up, and a smile lit her face. She beckoned them in with both hands.

They went over the wall and in by the back door. Nina embraced them.

'I thought you might have been arrested as well! I hardly slept a wink last night – neither did Oscar, I might tell you! He was worried sick. Did you see them take Oscar?'

They nodded.

'We had no warning, there was nothing we could do. Oscar was sitting here in the kitchen with me. We were having breakfast. I'd looked out into the street not ten minutes before, to see that the coast was clear. Suddenly the back door burst open, and in they came.'

'They came by the towpath?' asked Nik.

'Yes. I suppose it was foolish of me to think Oscar could be safe here. They were bound to track him down sooner or later. Even if he had been up in the attic they would have got him. They would have torn the house apart.'

'We always knew that,' said Nik.

'One of the policemen asked about you, Nik.'

'The tall one, with broad shoulders? Wearing a black reefer jacket?'

'That was him!'

'His name is Max!' said Nik, and he turned away to stare out of the window. The man was haunting him. He would see him again, he felt sure of that.

Nina told them Sophie and Jan hadn't come back last night, either. 'Let's hope they're safe! Not that anyone is safe. Oh, my poor Oscar!' Nina was overcome for a moment by a wave of tears and Lara moved to comfort her as she had done with Biba the day before.

'He will be in that terrible prison!' cried Nina. 'What will they do to him?'

'He'll be released tomorrow,' said Nik. 'Just you wait and see! The jail will be stormed!'

Seeing the expression on his face Lara thought he looked capable of storming it himself, single-handed.

SATURDAY

'I'm coming with you,' said Nina. 'I've no intention of staying at home to stir the pot today!' She untied the strings of the big apron that she put on in the mornings when she got up and took off at night when she went to bed. She hung it on a hook at the back of the kitchen door. 'This is more important than soup! I have to be there with everybody else. I have to be there when Oscar is set free.'

She opened the cupboard where she kept her odds and ends and took out two white, partially-burned candles and a small flag that had been carefully wrapped in soft paper. The candles she gave to Lara and Nik, along with tin lids, to use as holders. She herself would carry the flag. It was a little faded, but its stripes of red, white and yellow were still distinct. This had been the flag of their country before it was taken over by the regime.

Nina tucked the flag into her belt, underneath her shawl. She was ready! Lara and Nik had put on their new clothes.

They left the house soon after lunch. They'd had to eat before setting out. But naturally! Nina walked at a slower pace than did the young ones. She rolled a little, taking short steps. They had to hold themselves back.

'You two can go on ahead if you want to. You don't have to wait for an old slowcoach like me.'

'No, we're all going together.' Lara took Nina's arm, and Nik the other one.

Inevitably, their steps quickened again; it was difficult for Nik and Lara to contain themselves. They were buoyed up by excitement, like balloons filled with hot air. Lara felt as if only a thin cord held her to the ground and that if it were to be released she would take off up into the sky! Nina laughed, breathless, saying she felt as if they were carrying her along. At times her feet were scarcely touching the ground!

'It's all right! I don't mind. I like it. It feels like flying!'

By now, however, the streets were thronged and they had to moderate their pace to match the crowd's. There was a feeling of excitement, of expectation in the air. Some of the marchers carried long coloured streamers; a few played mouth-organs as they walked. Snatches of song could be heard. People spilled on to the roadway. Children clung to their parents' hands. The elderly clung to one another. It looked as if the city's whole population was converging on the centre. Lara was anxious in case there would not be room for everyone. They *must* get on to the square itself!

'It would be terrible to be left out, wouldn't it?'

'Don't worry,' said Nik, 'we won't be.'

There were police around, as they'd expected, but today they seemed to have been ordered to keep a low profile, at least for the present. They were standing by. At intersections and on corners, their big black vans waited.

The last kilometre into the centre was slow, and at times the huge seething mass of people came to a dead halt. The streets were jammed from wall to wall. Fathers lifted their small children on to their shoulders. Mothers held their babies protectively close. When at last they managed to nudge their way over the humped-back bridge into the square, they saw that the huge space was already three-quarters full. It was a few minutes after four. Long before six, it would be packed, as well as all the streets leading to it.

Then they saw the riot police.

Clad in helmets of grey-blue steel, riot shields in their left hands, batons in their right, they ringed the square. In front of the City Hall stood several rows of students with feet planted apart and arms linked right along the line. Not a chink of light showed between their arms. Facing them was a row of armed police. The police waited with their fire-arms presented, aimed straight at the students' chests. Their fingers rested on the barrels of their guns, ready to slide that last centimetre along the cold steel and pull back the triggers. And unleash a hail of death.

Lara looked at Nik in panic. Surely it was not going to be a re-run of last time! The scene came back to her in a sudden flash like an episode from a film. She could see the student mounting the lamp-post, hear him making his appeal, cut off by the sharp report that had sounded like the backfiring of a car. And then the student had slid silently down the lamp-post with a look of surprise on his face into the arms of the students below.

Nik was showing no emotion on his face, other than a slight pursing of the lips.

'Let's get nearer the front,' he said, taking Nina by the hand. She went with him docilely. In her kitchen she was the one who called the tune.

Lara followed on Nina's heels, trying not to tread on them. She knew Nik would have set his mind on getting as close as he could to the wall of students. He made it to the row immediately behind them.

'You're a determined boy!' Nina readjusted her kerchief, which had been knocked askew. 'I didn't think you could have slid a sheet of paper through a crowd as thick as that!' There was admiration in her voice.

She fumbled inside her shawl and brought out the little pennant. With a twist of her plump wrist she unfurled it and held it triumphantly aloft. She was not the only person in the crowd to be waving a flag.

And many, like Lara and Nik, carried candles that they would light once darkness fell.

Lara stood up on her toes. Her eyes travelled along the lines of students until she found the two heads she was looking for.

'There's Sophie! And Jan!'

'Praise be!' said Nina. 'At least that's one thing off our minds.'

Jan and Sophie had heard Lara. They looked round to wave and mouth a greeting. Then they turned back to face the police.

A frown puckered Nik's forehead. He was watching the balcony on the front of the City Hall and at the same time missing nothing that was happening around the square. He was noting the arrival of extra police, the swelling of the crowd, and the appearance of faces in the windows of the public buildings overlooking the square.

The faces were staying back from the windows, advancing only enough to be able to look down and study the crowd. Their heads were close together. They must be conferring. Deciding what action, if any, to take. They might be government ministers, chiefs in the police and army: people in power. But perhaps for not much longer. Nik knew, though, that they couldn't count on that. A hail of bullets would end all their hopes.

He continued to scan the faces of the crowd. Then he saw the one that he'd been expecting – fearing – to see, no more than ten metres from him.

Max was perched on the pedestal of a larger-than-life statue of the President's father, the founder of the regime. He thus stood elevated above the crowd. He was lounging against the statue's leg, resting one elbow on the fat, black marble knee. Even now, even here, in the midst of a crowd that would be against him and might even tear him apart, he wore an air of nonchalance.

He was looking straight at Nik.

Nik, although trembling a little, returned his gaze. Max had unfinished business with him. If the regime were to be toppled tonight, Max would not be able to complete it. But, on the other hand, if the police were to fire and the crowd to flee, Nik knew that then the secret policeman would be after him. With a vengeance. Max was a man who would not rest until he settled old scores.

Lara was also surveying the crowd, looking for known faces. She wondered where her priest would be. Not here, she considered. He would be in his little wooden church by the graveyard. She had a vision of him on his knees in a circle of candlelight, praying.

She spied Carl with a woman who must be his wife and gave them a wave. They returned her greeting, and Carl raised his thumb. They'd have to go and see Carl and explain about the bikes. Then Lara saw another face she recognized, one that surprised her. She nudged Nina.

'Look, it's our policeman!'

Nina twisted her head. 'So it is!'

They waved to him, and he raised both arms in the air in a triumphant gesture. He was in civilian clothes, and by his side stood a girl about the age of Lara. It must be Marta, the gymnastics champion.

The square was full now; people were lighting their candles, passing the flames along the rows. Lara and Nik took a light from a man in the row behind. It was nearing six o'clock and a fever was building. The chanting began.

Freedom! We want our freedom! Now!

The sound filled the air. As the crowd chanted it swayed, and the flags rippled overhead, making waves of colour, and the candles glittered like stars. The door at the back of the City Hall balcony remained closed.

Heads turned suddenly, one after the other, and the chanting slackened, then abruptly died. A student was climbing the lamp-post.

It was Jan!

SATURDAY: *6 p.m.*

Please God don't let Jan be shot! Lara gabbled inside her head. Please *don't!*

She reached for Nina's hand and they clung to one another, keeping their eyes trained on Jan.

Nik allowed himself a quick glance round in the direction of the statue. Max had abandoned his casual pose and was now standing to attention on the pedestal. Nik could tell all the man's senses were on alert and that he was braced for action. Or flight. But it seemed unlikely that Max would flee easily. He would put up a fight first. His right hand was in the bulging pocket of his jacket. His eyes were on Jan, as were the rest of the crowd's.

Jan had a tannoy in one hand; the other encircled the lamp-post. Below him stood several other students supporting his feet and legs.

'Fellow citizens,' Jan began, 'I have good news.

Great news!' His voice boomed out across the square. 'We have just been passed a message to say that the army has defected. It has come out for us, the people!'

The cheering that erupted was deafening. The crowd went mad. They jumped up and down and yelled and turned to hug one another, friends and strangers alike, and cheered again. The flags, the candles also, went into a frenzy.

Nik, though, was still watching Max. He saw his right arm move up, his hand emerge from his pocket, and with it something stubby and black.

'No!' yelled Nik.

In the same instant, another arm swerved upward in a high arc and came crashing down against Max's, knocking the revolver from his hand. The other arm belonged to Nina's friendly policeman.

Shouts and screams followed. Now there appeared to be a scuffle taking place down on the ground. The crowd eased back, to make a space around the wrestling bodies. Arms were seen flailing. Three men were down, as far as could be made out. Two surfaced from the mêlée, with tousled hair and red faces. They surfaced triumphant. One was a hefty-looking young man, the other the policeman. Between them, they had secured Max, who had ceased to struggle. He would know that ten thousand other people would be ready to take him on were his present captors suddenly to collapse.

As Max was yanked to his feet, he caught Nik's eye. His face was blank, like a screen that had been wiped clean. The crowd parted so that he could be led away.

There were still the riot police to consider. Nik saw that their eyes were wavering. They were no longer staring straight ahead impassively. It was plain that they didn't know what to do. And no one was coming out to tell them. They were at a loss. They continued to stand with their batons and shields presented, facing the hostile crowd.

Now several other students made a move, Sophie amongst them. Her pony-tail bobbed at the back of her neck. The students broke free from their ranks and charged the line of armed police. For a moment it looked as if the steel-helmeted men might resist, then they fell back and opened up their wall, almost with a shrug, as much as to say, 'What else can we do?' The students poured through the gap.

Half a dozen dashed for the City Hall, followed by Jan, who had scrambled back down from his lamp-post. The crowd watched anxiously. Would the students meet resistance inside? Where was the Chief of Police in his long grey coat and high black boots?

Where was the President?

Two minutes later, the door at the back of the balcony opened and out came the students with hands joined and arms raised high above their heads. Every man, woman and child in the square lifted *their* arms in salute and cheered afresh. Lara thought her throat would burst.

Jan addressed them again through the tannoy.

'News is coming in from all over the country. We have heard that the President has fled, but that is still a rumour, yet to be confirmed. But we *have* taken over the radio and television station.'

More cheers.

'So now we will be able to bring you the news – the real news! Two of our people, sadly, were shot and killed in the take-over.'

The crowd hushed.

'But apart from that, we know of no other loss of life. We still have work to do, however. It is not all over yet.'

'No, it's not.' Nik seemed to speak more to himself than anyone else. To Lara and Nina he said, 'I've got to leave you.'

'Where are you going?' demanded Lara.

He did not answer.

'You're going to the jail, aren't you? You are! Well, *I* am coming with you.'

SATURDAY: *7 p.m.*

There were several hundred people gathered in front of the prison. The big iron gates were wide open!

Lara slid her hand into Nik's. His fingers, after a moment's hesitation, fastened round hers. He would have liked to pretend that he could handle this on his own. But she sensed that he was glad to have her with him.

They edged round the side of the crowd, in the direction of the gate. People were chattering and laughing, and some were weeping. Isn't it wonderful? they were saying. Isn't it unbelievable? Lara could scarcely believe it herself. She felt as if she were moving through a dream. It had all happened so quickly, in the end. That was how revolutions often

131

did come about, Carl had told them; the authorities resisted for months, years, until there came a moment when they realized that they couldn't hang on any longer and their time was up.

Nik and Lara walked through the prison gates into the yard.

It was darker in the enclosed compound than it had been in the street. A few lamps placed around the high, gloomy brick walls shed a feeble, guttering light on the scene, creating deep shadows. Set into the walls were tier after tier of dirty, narrow windows, closed and barred. Most were dark; a meagre light shone at only a few. Behind one of these windows would be Nik's father. If he was still alive. And presumably, behind another, should be Oscar; or so they hoped.

The main entrance to the building also stood invitingly open. The guards must have fled. Some prisoners were coming out, in their drab grey uniforms and with their shaven heads. On the step, they paused to look up at the rectangle of sky visible above the rooftops. They shook their heads, as if in disbelief, then moved slowly towards the outer gate. A wave of cheers greeted them.

Nik and Lara entered the building. They were actually *inside* the dreaded top security jail! Lara shivered and let her shoulders curl up to her ears. The walls were grey, the ceiling was grey, the floor was grey. The place felt evil. It smelt thick and sour and of spilled blood. You could believe that terrible things had taken place here.

A rush of voices was coming towards them. They drew back against the wall automatically.

Round the corner came Jan and Sophie, with a

number of other students. In their midst was a familiar, flaming red head!

'Oscar!' Lara ran to meet him.

He looked tired and drawn and he had a bruise on his cheek and another above his left eye, but he was smiling. He embraced them both and lifted Lara clean off her feet.

Then he turned to the student beside him, a thin, dark young man, with several days' growth of beard fuzzing his chin.

'Nik and Lara, this is my great friend Stefan – Stefan Bild!'

Stefan shook hands with them both and said to Nik, 'I hear you came to call on me? I'm sorry I was not at home. Next time I shall be!'

Oscar asked about Nina. 'Is she all right? Is she safe?'

Nina was fine, they told him. Happy. Like everybody else. They'd left her in the square with some neighbours, making their way towards the cathedral. People were congregating in the church, to give thanks.

Nik did not look happy, though. Lara saw that he still wore his anxious air and his eyes were darting about restlessly.

'We're looking for Nik's father,' she said. 'But this is such a big place we don't know where to start.

'We'll help,' offered Sophie.

It was unlikely there would be any records left, said Oscar, so there was no point in their wasting time looking for them. Before absconding, the warders had built a large bonfire in the courtyard and burned stacks of papers.

Oscar took charge. He divided them up and gave each group a landing to cover. He told Nik and Lara to come with him.

At the end of the corridor they blinked as they came into a central well, blindingly lit by piercing white lights. Not even a fly could escape notice here. Ranged around the well were iron-balustraded gangways, one row above the other, and off the gangways were the heavy, studded cell doors. Tilting her head back to look upward Lara counted seven tiers.

'What is your father's name, Nik?' asked Sophie.

'Alexander.' Nik swallowed. 'Alexander Rand.'

Oscar led the way up the stairs, with Nik and Lara galloping at his heels. They were to do the first landing.

The doors had all been unlocked and a number of the cells were already empty. In others, men sat huddled, talking to one another and to relatives. They were free to go, but not yet ready to. They were trying to take in what had happened. Many looked ill and emaciated and some seemed close to death. They lay on filthy straw palliasses without moving, uttering low moans. In one cell a woman wailed over the inert body of a man. The stench in the little rooms was overwhelming. Brimming slop pails stood in corners. Cockroaches scuttled. As they worked their way along the landing, Nik's face looked grimmer and grimmer.

'Is there nothing we can do for them?' Lara appealed to Oscar.

'Someone will be along to help them,' he said gently. 'We'll be organizing ambulances to come from the hospital.'

He did not add that there would not be enough

134

working ambulances in the city to cope with all the emergencies. There was always a shortage, but tonight the pressure on them would be great. Jan had told Oscar that, as far as they knew, only two people had been killed, but many more had been injured. Police at the television and radio stations had put up resistance, as had the guards at a factory that workers had stormed.

They drew a blank on the first landing, went up to the second, which Jan and Sophie had checked out.

'No luck, I'm afraid, Nik,' said Jan.

'Not yet,' added Sophie, putting her arm round Nik's shoulder. 'But I'm sure he'll be in here somewhere. He's got to be, hasn't he?'

Unless he was dead. Lara tried to brush the thought from her mind. Nik's eyes were hollow.

The other students had done the third and fourth floors. Sophie and Jan said they would do the fifth, while Oscar, Lara and Nik made for the sixth. Their feet clattered on the stone steps and the noise echoed right up to the domed ceiling.

They worked their way again from cell to cell along the landing. By the time they came to the last door, Lara had almost given up hope. The pain building in Nik's eyes was evident. Her own throat felt tight and dry.

Oscar pushed open the door. The light from the gangway penetrated the room to show a man lying on a palliasse. His hair and beard were pebble-grey and his face a leaden colour, like that of dead ashes.

His eyes flickered open when they entered.

'Father!' The word rang out in the cell.

As Nik went forward to embrace his father, tears streamed down his face.

AFTERWARDS: *As told by Lara*

All that happened three months ago. It's June now, approaching high summer.

Yesterday was the anniversary of my mother's death. I went out to the graveyard to lay a wreath on her grave. Nina gave me a big armful of brilliant yellow and orange marigolds from her back garden.

'Here,' she said, 'take some sunshine with you! It'll be good for your mother's soul. And yours!'

It was a lovely bright day, the kind that makes you feel glad to be alive. Though I was feeling a bit sad, too, of course. How could I not? It's funny how you can be both happy and sad at the same time. Nina says life's made up of all shades and colours, like a rainbow that goes from dark to light. The dark makes you appreciate the light.

The birds were working away at full throttle in the high trees that border the cemetery. Between the graves the grass grew green and glossy. The graves themselves glowed with colour. Pansies, petunias, poppies, phlox, all were flowering in profusion. The old priest had been busy.

I put Nina's marigolds on my parents' grave and sat beside it for a while, talking to them in my head, and shedding a tear or two, then I went into the church. The priest was there, pottering about, dressed in a fusty-looking black cassock tied round the middle with a piece of string. He was polishing two ancient brass candlesticks. They're as old as the church itself. He'd kept them hidden away all these years.

136

'Look, Lara!' He held up the candlesticks for me to admire. 'Don't they shine like gold?'

His smile shone like gold, too. He's back in business again, as he puts it, since the Revolution. He's set up an altar, using a high narrow table and a yellowish-cream linen cloth. Nina and I have been to several of his services and each time the little church has been packed from wall to wall, with people spilling out on to the steps and path outside.

'This is a special day for you, isn't it?' He looked at me.

I nodded.

'Shall we light a candle for your mother? And say a prayer for her? And your father too – let's not leave him out!'

He fixed a tall white candle on a tin lid and placed it on the altar, then he stepped back to allow me to light it. My fingers trembled and I almost dropped the match. I closed my eyes while the priest prayed. Even through my closed eyelids I could see the golden flickering light.

I thought about the last three months.

Not everything has gone smoothly since that wonderful, incredible night in the square; one couldn't have expected it to. For the first few days we went round as if in a dream. We had one celebration after the other. Our street party was great fun. All the neighbours came, and Oscar was there, and Jan and Sophie and Stefan Bild. We had masses to eat and drink – everyone brought something – and two old men played music on their accordions for us to dance to. Then we lit a big bonfire on waste ground on the corner.

We stood watching the flames together, Nik and I, and he said, with a grin, 'Night fires burn brightest!'

Next day, he left with his father to travel up north. His uncle had come to fetch them in a van.

Once the celebrations were over, the problems began. Inevitable, said Oscar. People squabbled, and tried to grab power for themselves. When people smell power, it seems to make them crazed in the head, says Nina. And law and order (as it's called) has been difficult, with hardly any police left on the streets. (Our friendly policeman went back to his village, taking his family with him.) No one liked the police state when they had it but they don't like crime and vandalism either. It'll take a while, says Oscar, to get things sorted out and for everyone to settle down. You can't have a revolution and expect the country to run like clockwork straight away.

We're still short of food, and fuel, too, not that that matters quite so much now that it's summer, but they say next winter will be difficult. But, still, we're free! And that means a lot to us. We don't have to go around watching over our shoulders for the Black Berets and snoopers like Max. He's been locked up. As have the Crow and Dracula. They were found hiding in the loft of a remote farmhouse. The President and his closest advisors, including the Chief of Police, were arrested as they were trying to flee across the border. They're going to be rotting in jail for a very long time. None of us are weeping about that! And, in the autumn, we're to have elections. It's the first step on the road to democracy, says Oscar, but only a step. It's going to be a long, hard road.

Nina, as you might guess, is still making soup and brewing camomile tea when things get too hectic. I'm living with her full-time. Oscar lodges with her, too. He's back at the university, which has just re-opened. I'm attending the local school and enjoying it. I've been picked for the lower school basketball team and I'm learning to play the guitar. Oscar says there's no reason why I shouldn't go on to be a doctor. Our country badly needs doctors. Oscar's going to be an engineer, and build bridges. We need engineers as well. We need everything.

I've made new friends at the school but every Sunday I go back out to the orphanage and visit my old ones. Katya still tries to hang on to me when it's time to leave, but Biba says I've got my own life to lead and Katya has to understand that. Two new living-in nursery nurses have come to help Biba, so that is making life easier for her. And me. I don't feel so guilty now about not going back to the orphanage to live. It was a difficult decision for me. Both Biba and Nina stood back and let me make it on my own. They said I had to consider my future, so that was what I did.

And tomorrow, I'm going to see Nik! I'm to spend two whole months up in the mountains with him and his father and grandparents. I've never been up north. Oscar tells me the wild flowers are fantastic on the high meadows; they look like shimmering carpets of colour spread across the ground.

When summer is over Nik is to come back with me to the city. He wants to go to school too so that he can study afterwards at the agricultural college and learn how to manage the land properly. The farms are all in a dreadful state because they've been ill treated. The soil's been abused and the machinery allowed to rust and fall to bits.

I'm so excited I can hardly wait until tomorrow. I can't wait to see Nik. Before he went off with his father, he told me that I was his best friend and always would be. Coming from him, that was something! I didn't know what to say, for once! I just looked at him and he gave me that lopsided grin of his. And I felt warm inside.

When I open my eyes, I see that the candle is burning with a steady flame.